I0650766

ISBN 978-0-9978175-1-5

Printed in the United States of America

The Homeland Security Chronicles

Warren Dent

Acknowledgments

My writing group has been a constant source of review and critique on the stories contained in this collection. I thank them for their insistence on 'showing', not 'telling' wherever possible.

My wife, Gail Monica, has put up with incomplete, misspelled, and poorly expressed first drafts, and has energetically Americanized strange Australian expressions and idioms.

Thanks to all.

Author's Note

There are four stories here. Three relatively short, one much longer. The first and second stories are about 15 pages each, the third one only 9 pages. The final story has 13 chapters and takes up 75 pages.

Please note that the final story basically includes the content of the first story and some of the third story plus much, much more. If you only have time or interest for really shorter tales, just read the first three.

If you have more time, simply ignore the first story and read the remaining three. The final story – Massive Catch – is the most creative and comprehensive.

You can find my website at www.krandis.com . My email address is warren@krandis.com

Dedication

To all the wonderful females in the world who serve in our security forces. May the future be as potentially challenging to you as I have assumed in the stories herein.

The Homeland Security Chronicles

Warren Dent

Table of Stories

Standard Operations

<u>Classified/Homeland Security (map attached).</u>

<u>Case: i9-4579</u>

The banshee wail of the intruder alert sets my scalp tingling. I yell. "Where's the source Priscilla?"

"Strait of Georgia ma'am, just southwest of Vancouver. Looks like the city is place of origin."

"I turn to my 2IC. "Anna, get a drone out there, stat."

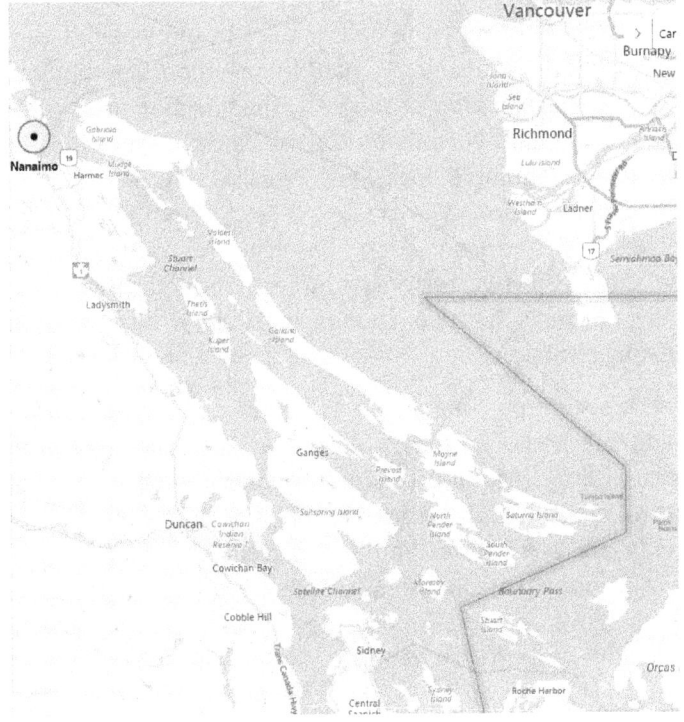

"On it Cap'n." The prowler she selected lifts off the front deck with a giant whoosh.

I should have known Anna would be ahead of me. The gal is extraordinary. A week new to our station at Roche Harbor, but already acting like a veteran. Incredibly fit, agile as a monkey, strong, keen as they come. Fiery red hair masking an amazing intellect. I love her enthusiasm and zest for her job. She already has the dock lines loosened on the port side as I start the five giant outboards. 1000 horsepower come to life with a tremendous roar, temporarily drowning out further conversation. The all-round rubber inbuilt fenders stretch and screech as I pull away.

This is no time to obey the harbor rules of 'no wake'. I gun the Mercs to half capacity. A giant plume shoots up behind us. As we reach the outer markers, the intruder siren goes off again. My ears go into protective block mode. What is going on? A multiple invasion? Priscilla yells across the cockpit. "Nanaimo. Makes no sense." Another drone launches from the front deck. The big screen in the main cabin shows the two terrorist source spots with bright red flashing circles, the two drones with thick blue arrows indicating direction.

I tap the secure personal audio nodule in my throat. "Calling Canada SeaLand. Come in." I flip the silver Encompassing Communication Module out of the breast pocket on my uniform, and throw it to Priscilla. She secures the link to our compatriots in Victoria, and the big screen splits in two vertically. John Larson's image appears on the right side showing him standing beside his desk. I tap the nodule again so our conversation is shareable.

"Hi Katherine. We think you can anticipate more of these alerts coming in any second. Canada Inland Intel has been warning us for a week about increased hot-spot dialog between cells. They're trying to identify sources ahead of launch. Don't depend on it. Over."

John is a good guy. Land-based though. Canadian defense policy is not as intense as ours, and the country openly relies on our resources, especially in these boundary waters.

"Thanks John, will let you know what we find." The blast of the siren once again drowns out whatever John says in response. I shout. "Geez Priscilla, can we shut it down a notch? I'll be deaf before I'm thirty." She reacts slowly and I realize she is concentrating on Larson's picture on the video display. She pivots toward me, one hand clamped on her crotch. "God that guy's got a great big bulge in his pants. Sure would like to help him get dressed."

Despite the urgency of the mission I turn so she can't see my reaction, and smile. Twenty-five years ago men would have lost their jobs if they'd made analogous remarks over a gal's boobs. Boy, had things switched around in the intervening time. No more glass ceilings through which to look up skirts, rather there are discreet wearable digital screens that check any man's measurements within 15 feet. I turn back, feign a look of disinterest, and ask loudly, "Come on gal, what's that latest source? Get your clit under control. We obviously have a pending crisis here." I know a lot about Priscilla's body. We'd been lovers for over a year now.

"Point Roberts, Kath." She is lazy about names but I don't really mind. "Right under the noses of our station there. Bloody daring jerks. Clearly a diversion effort. Which one of these three sources is the real McCoy?"

The siren shrieks again. "Hell, four of the bastards, not three. Origin is Ganges, of all places. Backwater retirement town. There goes the last of Anna's drones Kath. Wanna call SkyLock?"

I hesitate. We'd had runs against us before, involving two terrorist vessels. Four suggests a heightened sense of urgency on the part of the militants to get another illegal terrorist across the border. How many of these boats on the water are decoys? How many are real? Clearly we can't apprehend all four. The four detected have been picked up by the signals emanating from concentrated intensity electronic communication devices. Our high-def intelligence alert systems have been aware of these for some months now.

Damned terrorists. If the terrorists knew how easily we can pick them up now, they'd take advantage of it. They'd tie up our resources with fake decoys, then send the important guy in a regular boat with no bristling antennae. Just a sporty innocent runabout. We'd never catch him.

I decide against contacting SkyLock directly. In a way they are already involved. It is their satellites which have identified the four possible terrorist boats. We could ask them for more intelligence, but we are busy enough. Needing a short conference, I ease the engines on our 40 foot runner back from our 50 knot speed. "What do you think Anna?" A brilliant mind hidden behind all those red ringlets, I have no trouble deferring to her. She has a high forehead for intellect, and an athleticism that is awesome to watch in motion. I haven't gotten to learn the intricacies of her body yet, but I will in time. God she's attractive.

"First, forget Point Roberts. I think they're playing with us. They know full well that anything unusual in town would have been spotted already. No, that one's just a one-man show to irritate us. As for Vancouver, I don't mind betting that the organization's headquarters is in town, but launching from there is just too obvious. It's the Ganges and Nanaimo sources that are new. Nanaimo is much further away. As we sit right now on the edge of Haro Strait, we have lots of options."

I scan the Strait ahead. A heavy freighter is coming up from the south, and white caps indicate there is a strong wind creating two-foot plus waves. Nothing our boat can't handle. Might be a bit bumpy, that's all.

I turn to the screen. "John, any views contrary to Anna's?"

Bouts of annoying pixilation violate the image on his half of the device's veneer. All we hear is "… trying to learn more about Nanaimo boat." Bandwidth is often an issue in the Strait.

I have an idea. "Anna, suppose the Ganges boat knows we'll engage them and is set to keep us busy checking them out for half an hour or more while the Nanaimo boat sneaks into Stuart or Patos Island say, turns off their equipment, and transfers their cargo to an innocent runabout? Possible?"

"I like your thinking boss," pipes up Priscilla, although I'd asked Anna. "And it gives me another idea. Let's intercept the boys from Ganges. I have a new electronic gadget you may not know about that could be useful. Got it yesterday. Here." She removes her Maui Jim's, one of the few brands of sunglasses that have lasted all this time, and retrieves from the pocket pouch on her left trouser leg a small metallic cube, sides about an inch long, with a sophisticated click switch on one face.

"Cool. What does it do?" Anna asks.

"Negates certain communication protocols. It's called a Selective Communication Device or SCD. Once we pull alongside the Ganges boat, I can take a read of all the comm. standards they are using with my personal wrist machine, and set SCD to block any outward use of those protocols, while not interfering with incoming messages. Sort of a jamming device that can be one way or two way."

"What's the advantage?" Anna asks.

"Well, I can set it so they can still get messages from their people but will wonder why they can't respond. The tricky part is that I have to get it onto their boat and hide it as it's an Extended Near Field Communication based system. It's small enough to stay concealed unless a really thorough scrub is made of the boat. Once onboard and active, we can speed off to intercept the Nanaimo boat carrying what we hope is the real prize and they can't let headquarters know any concerns."

Anna responds. "If these guys are like all the others we've apprehended we shouldn't have a problem. They're mere males, leery jihadist creeps, craving feminine recognition, visual and verbal."

"What do you have in mind?" I ask.

Anna turns to Priscilla. "Are you willing to parade a nice big dose of cleavage under their eyes? You have the best offering among us. While they ogle you, I'll drop the device in one of the main cabin's side storage pockets among their unused fishing tackle or somewhere else innocuous. Dumb pricks."

Priscilla makes me smile. "Happy to show off the ladies anytime… "

I move the throttle forward, loving the sound of the highly tuned mercs as they churn the foam filled water behind us. We start bouncing almost immediately. "Let's intercept these guys near the southeast end of Moresby Island before they cross the international border. They'll bitch that we're out of our jurisdiction but we'll pretend their GPS is faulty. John will support us. Priscilla, what is that drone telling us about a possible contact point?" While Priscilla fiddles with her wrist machine, John's affirmation of support comes through loud and clear. No more pixilation disturbance on the screen.

"You need to slow down 10 knots Kath, and it will work out perfectly. And listen-up you bi-sexed comrades, keep your eyes on the waterway as I enhance my killer offerings." I recognize that Priscilla has deliberately taken a bit of a risk with her labeling. We aren't quite sure of Anna's sexual preferences yet, although hopeful she is at least bi. We figured males wouldn't be able to stay away. How she responds to both them and females we still need to learn.

I refocus my mind. Right, drop speed. I adjust the throttles and watch as Priscilla shakes loose her light brown hair. It had been pulled back into a small stub per official guidelines, but now falls a few inches below her shoulders. She undoes three buttons on her blouse revealing a gorgeous set of suntanned 36D's that I've always envied. And I know from experience that she can present them in incredibly enticing ways.

Oh yes, if these decoy terrorists are like their foreign predecessors - fascinated by women unadorned in full-cover black - then they are dead ducks when they meet Priscilla.

*   *   *

The two dark complexioned men smirk as we pull alongside their Trophy sport. We explain our interest in checking their craft for safety features. Both sides know the reasoning is farcical, and the terrorists play their role dutifully, complaining about the location, and the unnecessary stoppage since their boat is new.

They are taken aback when I ask "Why do you have so many communication masts and antennas?" They have no good answer other than "personal preference in managing broad ranging environmental information and long-distance communication both within Canada and across the border." The three of us smile at the canned response.

We check the intruder boat's supply of flares and personal safety devices and declare we have no concerns, congratulating the owners on a well-managed boat. Priscilla returns from checking the anchor locker near the bow of their twin-engined 30 foot cuddy cabin vessel. She has to step down from the front deck into the main cabin. She leans forward, stretching out her arm to one of the men to aid her stability. As reward he gets a magnificently memorable view of Priscilla's golden orbs. His friend hastens forward to also help.

Regretfully, for she's enjoying the interaction, Anna turns her head away and drops the SCD into a small pocket under one of the back cushions. She and Priscilla leave the boat and wave goodbye to the two goggle-eyed foreigners.

Our laughter finally subsides as we imagine the men's frustration trying to tell their friends about the good looking agents they encountered. I push the throttle forward and steer northeast, wanting to get to a convenient hiding place to lay in wait for the Nanaimo boat. I ask Anna for a recommendation.

Anna consults the feedback from the drone 1000 feet above the Nanaimo terrorist boat. The boat is heading down the inside passage rather than outside Valdes and Galliano islands in the Strait of Georgia. Anna makes a calculated guess that it will stay north of the Pender islands, suggesting east Camp Bay and Blunden Islet as possible hiding spots for us. Even if the terrorist boat elects to run south of the Penders we'll be in a formidable chase position.

Under Anna's guidance we end up idling on the south side of Blunden Islet. It's a full five minutes before the planned encounter with the foreign boat. We are still in Canadian waters, a little over a mile northwest of the border. We've turned off all electronics so that we provide no discernible signature in case we are being tracked. We've even shut down communication with the drone above the terrorist boat since the last signal was exactly as we had expected. Priscilla asks, "What's our strategy Kath? Fast chase with full lights, siren, and electronic interference? Or silent tracking to destination?"

I think for a few seconds, then respond, "I don't want any chance for these bastards to land anyone. When they do that, it's all the harder for our local forces to catch them. So it's full bore ladies. The works. Nothing spared. We go after them max force. No holds barred. You both OK with that?" Two heads nod yes.

Anna queries, "Weapons?"

"Laser guns. Head shots only if they draw on us. Priscilla, your turn to stay hidden below, so they think there's only the two of us. You both know the drill. I've got both good and bad vibes about this. Their course shows no evasive maneuvers such as zig-zags, or random stops. They came through Dodd Narrows rapids as if they were a tourist boat. I think these guys are acting innocently, wanting us to think they are like any other sports boat out here bent on enjoying the international waters. But I think there's a terrorist below deck. Two minutes till they come by. Throttles up in neutral in one minute. Stand by."

A new blue Cobalt R35 streaks into the waters 200 yards ahead of us. Nice boat, sleek lines, hard top, no bimini, two men silhouetted in the driving seats, multiple antennae originating near the windshield arced backwards. We spring out behind them in full intercept regalia. Anna focuses the high-tech laser gun located on our arch at their rear end where the inboard motor sits churning the waters ahead of us. We're seen and they pick up speed, crossing the border 100 yards ahead of us.

Unexpectedly, they slow down and turn 90 degrees to port. Anna gets it immediately. "They realize they're in U.S. waters and are turning to head back into Canadian territory. Can you cut them off?"

I smile. This is where I excel. I know my blood pressure is ramping up but I actually feel icy calm and controlled. Unlike our target, I don't slow down an iota, but pull a 2G port turn, the two starboard engines' props lifting above the water surface and screaming their dislike. Anna and Priscilla hang on tightly. When we settle back on equilibrium I'm on a course nearly parallel to our foreign friends and only 50 yards in arears. They skim by Skipjack Island, headed north towards the tip of Saturna. I push the throttle forward to the maximum and in 30 seconds we are alongside, Anna hailing them with the electronic megaphone, telling them to pull over.

They ignore us, which gives me new rights. I have no hesitation jamming the full starboard rubber fender against their frame, jolting them severely. It's a risky move since they could bounce back and partially lift out of the water, cutting into our rear frame. The training films are clear, but this is my expertise. The foreigner in the passenger seat turns white, not believing our intensity. He shouts to his companion to stop. To no avail. They plough on, but their boat is now turned northeast, and will have difficulty getting back into Canadian waters, especially since the border becomes true northward between Tumbo and Patos Islands.

"Fire at their engine area Anna." She does and black smoke emanates from the fiberglass cover. Their boat slows, and for good luck I make another bruising assault between the driving position and the bow. They get the message and shut down. We pull alongside and listen to a litany of curses, complaints, and threats, some in English, most in a foreign language.

We tie up alongside as the smoke from the destroyed engine dwindles and dies to a limp hissing stream. We show our credentials and ask the two men why they tried to avoid us and ignored our request to stop. These guys are less articulate than those in the Ganges boat. They struggle with English and make little sense with their replies. Surprising, as most of the terrorists we encounter have been well trained in our language. One of the men guards access to the downstairs cuddy cabin. We figure we know why. Anna steps to his side and removes the boat's keys from the ignition, dropping them in her pants pocket. Sergio, the guy standing in the main cabin, and whose name we learn later, reaches out and cries, "Our property! Give back."

Anna looks at him with disdain, and says, "When we're done, shitface. Passports?" Sergio's face clouds over. I figure he's looking for a fight. He's a bull of a man. Over six feet tall, broad shoulders, chest like a barrel, black hair brushed forward and upwards. Physique of a weight-lifter. His face changes into a threatening scowl.

He surprises us both by leaping from his boat to ours, probably intent on breaking something aboard. However, the tables are turned as Priscilla rises from the companionway and delivers a hard sharp kick to the man's groin. He groans and doubles over, clutching his vitals. His stamina is evident however, as he draws himself upright and lunges forward. Mistake. Priscilla takes a step back, and with a perfect martial arts maneuver, kicks him under the chin. His head snaps back and he drops like a sack. Go woman, go! She jumps on him, turns him over, pulls his arms behind him and cuffs him with the new electronic grips. He starts yelling, at which point she jams the mouth lock between his teeth where it clamps onto both his lips and teeth and silences him.

"All under control boss," she tells me. The cowardly passenger, still shielding access to the cuddy, quickly hands over his passport. Abdul something or other. Passport in Arabic. I don't bother to check it further, but indicate he should move away from the door frame. He resists, shaking his head 'no' back and forth. I'm tired of the resistance, and notion to Anna to do her thing. Her chance to get physical. Why not? Get the frustrations out after the tense chase. The rule book is deliberately vague about physical interaction. Written by women of course. We love it. It gives us a lot of freedom that wasn't there in the old days.

I stand back thinking the idiot guarding the door has no idea what he's in for. The dummy has his arms outstretched across the entryway. Anna's first punch jams into his solar plexus. His arms drop. The next punch is a hook under his chin. His eyes roll around in their sockets and he literally crumples to the floor. Anna reaches down to move his body out of the way.

A strong hair-covered arm pulls her into the cuddy. She yelps in pain as the arm's owner smashes her on the shoulder with the butt of a black pistol. He pokes it forward, aiming it directly at me.

I duck behind the driver's seat, wary of the gunman's intent. Does he plan to use Anna as a hostage, or is he going to shoot his way out with her as his shield? In the instant I deliberate, there is a sharp 'zap' sound and the gunman's pistol goes flying, his fingers dangling uselessly. Markswoman Priscilla to the rescue. I jump forward and apply a headlock to the infidel and pull him over Anna's body out of the cuddy cabin. He reaches up with his good hand, grabs my hair and yanks. "Yow." My head jerks back but I refuse to give up my grip. Next thing I know Priscilla delivers a karate chop to the man's throat and he goes limp.

We bind the three shits into immobility, and pull a sling for Anna's right arm out of our first-aid kit. I establish comms with John in Victoria and with our headquarters back at Roche. We retrieve the drones and secure them in their small hangars forward. We send images of the three passports ahead, and secure the terrorists' Cobalt hard against our starboard fender.

All three of us feel drained. Good reason. Usually our intercepts don't become so physical.

We spend time making sure our versions of the whole exchange are consistent. The chips planted in our necks will be examined to check we went by the rules - our only possible indiscretion being the safety check of the Ganges boat in Canadian waters. I have no doubt, however, that John Larson will stand by his approval for us to proceed.

I take us home at half speed, sensitive to minimizing bumps that might aggravate Anna's discomfort. I shouldn't have worried, I guess, for the mild painkillers we'd administered are doing their job well.

We're met at the dock by a cadre of uniformed agents. They happily take our prisoners away. We bathe in the well-wishes and congratulations coming our way, recounting our intercept several times. We know there'll be a de-briefing later, but for now it's rest and recover time. I look at my two subordinates, grateful for their support and commitment.

"You two are positively awesome. Simply the best there is. I'll go anywhere with you."

Anna smiles. "Good," she responds. "I need a shower. Care to join me?"

Out of Scope

Classified/Homeland Security (map attached)

The sharp buzz in my ears told me headquarters was trying to contact me. I tapped my throat nodule and uttered, "Katherine, standing by."

"Hi Kath." David's voice bounced off a bone inside my head somewhere and my body went to full alert. Rarely did David call, and so early in the morning? We three girls had just arrived at our boat, hadn't even unpacked our small backpacks, so I wondered what was up. "Can you guys head up to the office here?"

Like I'd say 'no'? "Be there shortly." I turned to Priscilla and Anna. "David wants us in the office. Let's unpack later." Hmmm. No extra information. Were we in for some sort of disciplinary chat? Did we have a new assignment? Was one of us to be moving on? We jumped over the rubber fenders to the dock, fresh and energetic, ready to face the day which was dawning under pink clouds. A devious thought crossed my mind. "Anna, you left that Statvibe behind right?" The latest version of her male analyzer device we'd all seen in action. "Still unpacked darn it, boss," she replied. "Too damned bad, we don't see David up close and personal too often." He was the commander of our division, rarely in town.

God-damned woman, Anna. Sex-crazy. "Didn't you get any last night?" I asked. "I'll never tell," she replied. Priscilla snickered. Oh, yeah, guess they'd been together.

"Come on, close ranks here, attitude adjustment, we're off to visit the big man." He was probably watching through binoculars. I bet he liked what he saw. We were three 23-27 year olds serving the country through Homeland Security in the U.S./Canadian border waters. Miscellaneous sea duties.

Had a very fast outboard-driven intercept boat under our command. We were top of the line in our class of recruits, had been together nearly two years. All excellent swimmers, shooters, and martial arts proponents. Usually with an added element, called 'female surprise', as we apprehended terrorists, smugglers, drunken boat drivers and worse.

We picked up our pace along the outer dock at Roche Harbor, silently enjoying the admiring looks from fisherman and tourists up early. Some checking their gear, others stretching their legs and sipping from mugs of hot coffee. The water was placid, although the pink sky didn't auger well. Windy day ahead. Wind was always the worst hazard on the seas.

One small wolf-whistle told us our slacks and blouses were nice and tight. Off duty, all three of us maintained rigorous work-outs at the local gym. We certainly deserved that time-tested call of male appreciation.

David had hot tea ready for me, and hot coffee for my companions. An open box of donuts was tempting, but we passed on the sugary fat providers. David's craggy looks belied his age which we guessed at early forties. A shock of thick dark hair, wide-set eyes in an attractive face. And a booming voice.

"Good morning ladies, I have a very unusual request for your services. Hear me out now. Our Canadian counterparts, with their primarily land-based force, have been approached by the Royal Canadian Mounties to help solve a growing problem in their tourist waters. Prostitution!"

"Hardly a Homeland Security issue David. And nothing that new," I suggested.

"Hold it Kath. Let me finish. Yes, one of the revenue sources for the wide-ranging water-taxis up north is delivering girls to resorts. Every now and then the police crack down and arrest some gals, but it doesn't take long before activity picks up again. There are more violent and important crimes that occupy the police's priorities most of the time."

"So what's different this time?" Priscilla asks.

"Well the gals are somewhat more sophisticated these days. It seems there's at least one group that has its own boat. They not only visit resorts, but drop anchor in popular tourist spots. The message gets around and 'Johns' take advantage of the ease of access. There's been one death of a client due to a drug overdose, and of course lots of complaints from families having fun with their kids there."

Anna, the thoughtful one, prods further. "How can these gals afford boats? Perhaps the boats are owned by a friend or pimp and 'loaned out'. Or, worse, some bad-news mafia-type organization is financing the whole offering, spurring drug sales. Shit, what a mess."

"You got it," David adds. "Which is why you folks come into the picture. The cops in Campbell River have easy-to-notice police boats. Like yours. But we also have our Meridian 541 flybridge, which looks like most other flybridges from a distance. Would not be conspicuous in the popular coves up north."

"Fine," I said, "but we have no jurisdiction north of the border. All we could do is observe and identify locations."

"The Canadian authorities are willing to provide you with police powers for the exercise. In fact I have your shields and written engagements right here." David holds up a large packet marked with dark official ink stamps over the front. "Your job, should you accept it, is to arrest as many of these prostitutes as you can find. Canadian Police will meet you at any arrest rendezvous and take care of things from there on. I must admit I feel proud that your reputation has spread so far north, but I made no commitment to your taking on the request. What do you say?"

Priscilla speaks up first. "I haven't been to Desolation Sound in years. I guess most of our work would be at night. If that means I can add to my suntan during the day I'll be happy to sign up. Doesn't sound as dangerous as some of the other activities we've been involved in. And sure would be different. How long would this be for? Just a few days or longer? Anna, Katherine?"

"I'm more concerned with some of the logistics," Anna states. "Can the Homeland Security decals be removed from our boat? Can we add a rear high intensity searchlight? What's the policy on allowing us to carry stun and laser guns, and handcuffs? Can we have a rifle to disable the outboard engines on an inflatable a client is using to get away? What about a supply of GPS trackable devices to attach to suspect boats? Jamming equipment? Extra tow ropes? Scuba tanks? There are probably other things we need that I can't think of this moment. If we can get all those things, I'm happy to go along. As Priscilla says, certainly a different type of assignment. Kath?"

"No way I'm letting you two go without me. Guess we're saying 'yes' David. We'll need updated detail charts for the area of course, and all those things Anna listed. Possible?"

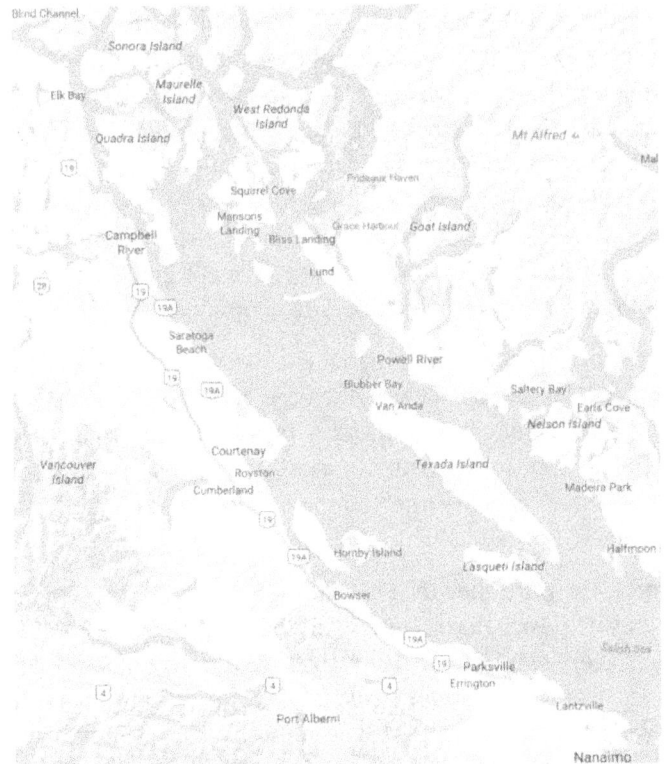

"Charts are being downloaded as we speak. I sort of guessed you gals would have a hard time refusing. It'll take time to outfit the boat with all the other requests however.   In any event you'll all need to get civilian clothes, so why don't you take the morning to get prepared, buy food and drink for your trip, and we'll plan on a 2pm departure.   And remember, while the sun will be warm during the day, the nights can be quite cool up there, so take appropriate outfits."   We all murmured our acknowledgments. "Thanks ladies. You're the best. I need to let my Canadian friends know."

*   *   *

As predicted, the wind has picked up substantially by the time we depart. Driving the flybridge with its superstructure takes some getting used to. Our normal cruiser has a much lower center of gravity and is built for speed. This two storey lady is built for comfort. We leave the bimini top down and are navigating from the inside cabin. Our timing for Dodd Narrows is way off slack water time so we plough through against a 7 knot current, get shoved around a bit, but not unsafely. We pull into Nanaimo just after 5pm, having averaged about 16 knots along the way.

Next morning, we are up early, and head northwest into the Salish Sea for Campbell River. The wind is weaker than yesterday but the waves are in our face, so it takes us just over 5 hours to conquer the nearly 80 nautical miles. We radio in from a couple of miles out and are met at the marina by two burly local policemen, Ron, and Stuart.

Over a late lunch they tell us what they know. The brothel boat, as they've designated it, tends to move to a new anchorage or resort every two to three days. Their main source of information comes from local street prostitutes who indicate there is a growing market at sea. The police also hear from mothers and fathers who tend to call in using their cell phones when they see suspicious activity on a neighboring boat anchored in the same bay as them. Two or more visiting inflatables and loud laughter and music are the usual reasons,

although extended families and groups often rendezvous in Desolation Sound, so such gatherings are not fool-proof of any wrong-doing.

It's presumed the pros communicate with some land base by cell phone, although reception in the area is spotty. It's also possible that they talk very briefly or in code with past clients on one of the lower number VHF channels. The police have not been able to pick up any such messages, although they are generally too far away to expect to do so.

Late last week, a client of the pros nearly drowned when he smashed his homeward-bound zodiac onto rocks in the Octopus Islands, and had to be rescued by a 'Vessel Assist' responder. In his drunken state the guy talked about tying up at a big Bayliner and joining a party involving a number of female swingers, one of whom he paid for services. Similar, isolated, but corroborating stories and reports had been turning up randomly all through summer.

Based on the contact from Vessel Assist, the next morning after the accident, Ron and Stuart commandeered a helicopter and raced to the area. About 5 miles away from the accident location they spotted a large pilothouse Bayliner, about 50 feet long, heading for the Yuculta and Gillard Rapids possibly on its way to Dent Island resort. They called the resort and the dockmaster confirmed he was holding a reservation made just the day before for a boat of the size indicated. Of course Bayliners are the Chevrolet of boats – the most common brand on the waters – so no guarantees of course. Still, it was the most likely target of the moment.

Dent Island resort is an upscale salmon fishing resort offering 'luxury in the wilderness', including non-fishing scenic adventure tours and wildlife viewing boat tours. It boasts superb dining, a full service marina and internet access. Access to the island is governed by the behavior of three rapids in surrounding waters, so boats tend to arrive in groups at slack water times. We jointly decide the resort will be our initial destination.

Three hours and a little less than 40 nautical miles later, we arrive. A pleasant young man at the resort dock grabs the midcraft line Anna throws to him and secures it around the low wooden dock rail. Priscilla jumps off the stern and ties us down loosely, as I ease the bow thruster gently to port, bringing us parallel and tight to the dock. "Well done ladies, you did that nicely. Welcome to Dent Island. I'm Doug, the dockmaster. We have 50v power for you, water for washing only, not potable. Let me know if you need anything else. Are you thinking about dinner in the lodge, or are you eating on board? I'm sure there's room on our top deck if you'd like to sample our first-class cuisine."

I have no doubt that the same thoughts as mine are occurring in Priscilla and Anna's minds. Who knows when we may hit a resort again. "Can't wait to try a great dinner. Would 7 pm work?"

"If that's a problem, I'll let you know. Glad to have you here."

*   *   *

In the ante-room to the dining area, there's a small library, and a large telescope pointing out the window past the marina and across the water to Big Bay. An old mahogany desk sports a monitor attached to a PC, obviously meant for guest use. Priscilla wanders over, humming thoughtfully. "Got an idea ladies. Wonder if our targets 'advertise'. While we're

waiting for dinner I'll try some random searches, and see if I get any meaningful hits."

Anna and I stand behind her watching as she opens a browser and elects the GoogHoo search engine. She tries a number of inputs, 'Campbell River escorts,' 'Desolation Sound parties,' 'Male sea services,' 'Fun in Desolation Sound,' 'Good times on the water,' 'Girl tease northern waters', and 'Extra resort services.' No uptake.

I'm impressed with her imagination. Anna and I throw in our suggestions. 'Extra hunter experiences', 'Salmon fishing plus,' 'Parties on the waters,' 'More than a water-taxi.' All to no avail. Our boat name is called, indicating our dinner table is ready. I suggest one last input as Priscilla starts to stand up. 'Desolation Sound girls'. This time a full screen comes up showing four pretty silicon enhanced bare breasted girls in enticing poses on the rear and upper decks of a large boat. Eureka. We've hit gold. Priscilla quickly shuts down the site as two other couples enter the room, and we follow the maitre'd to a table out on the wooden deck that overlooks the side rapids and marina. The setting is beautiful, making us forget our internet finding, and instead, concentrate on the spectacular view in front of us.

A couple of fishing boats come roaring up the side rapids, and a bald eagle alights in a tree at the end of the verandah. We stare mesmerized. A small seaplane bisects our view to the south and we watch it float gently to a landing and taxi in to the special short dock, where two passengers alight and are met by owners of one of the moored yachts. Thirty minutes later the four are seated at a table next to us.

Our dinner setting is absolutely serene. It defines a sense of tranquility that doesn't occur in the days of our regular duties. In this place, everything is right with the world. Fish jump, birds cry, water cascades over rocks with a soothing sweeping sound. The service and food are superb, and we are transported to a wilderness nirvana none of us have ever experienced before. There's little talk at any of the tables. We're all in another world.

*　　　*　　　*

Back on our boat we eventually find our voices. Anna boots up a laptop, types in the password we've been given for the resort's guest Wi-Fi use, and pulls up the site for 'Desolation Sound girls'. Pretty blatant is all I can say. No question that we've hit on an advert for our quarry. There are a couple of give-aways. First, there's a limited calendar. Just two entries for the next four days, Prideaux Haven and Grace Harbour. Does that mean one boat going to two places, or two boats moored separately, one in each location? The website is not that sophisticated to be able to tell. Crap, both locations are well south of where we're currently located.

The other give-away is less obvious. We wondered out loud how clients would find the girls since the boat appeared to be a fairly common Bayliner 4588 PilotHouse. Anna, looking more closely, notices that one of the girls' arms is outstretched, seemingly pointing to a small blue and white triangle, each side probably no more than six inches long, on the starboard side fiberglass molding just under the upper deck. Relatively inconspicuous and easily overlooked by the casual observer. Anna suggests there's probably one on the other side of the boat as well.

We flip a coin to choose our rendezvous for tomorrow. Prideaux Haven it is. This is a large well-protected waterway, encompassing a finger bay named Melanie Cove. No trouble to anchor, raft, or stern-tie fifty boats or more in the two bays. We try to call Ron and Stuart at Campbell River, but fail to connect. Apparently our cell provider doesn't have service in the area. We sit upstairs on the bridge savoring the left-over remnants of a second bottle of Cabernet Sauvignon we didn't quite finish at dinner. So peaceful. Unreal. Faint kids screams on a couple pf the other boats fail to interrupt our reverie.

Near lunchtime next day we find a nice stern-tie position in Melanie Cove that has just been vacated. We've decided to get some serious tanning in for a few hours before taking the zodiac out to look for our target boat. Priscilla has already had the binoculars out and made several weeps around the bay, but there are too many small coves and rocky points to see everything, and she has no luck. We switch into our bathing suits. That is, Anna and I put our bikini bottoms on and head for the bow deck. Priscilla wants an overall tan and heads for the upper deck, au naturel. I can't help noticing that she has a new landing strip. Two parallel well-defined lines perhaps an inch or so apart. I compliment her, and she tells me it's in response to a male friend's request. Ah, to be bi.

Late afternoon we take a spin around the large bay, three gals out enjoying the waning sunshine. We have light jackets on, and it doesn't take long to find the Bayliner with the triangle emblem. All quiet at the moment, no-one visible. Perhaps the girls are still sleeping, or inside putting chips and hors d'oevres together, or simply reading. We keep our distance and return to our anchorage and prepare to heat up small frozen pizzas. A far cry from the delights of the previous evening. I try my cell again, and get 1 bar of reception. I try a text message to Ron, rather than a voice call, and he responds. Super! I indicate where we are located, and that we're watching a boat at the west end of the bay. He agrees to stand by till 11pm in case we get successful.

That's a relief, as I had wondered how we'd get in contact if our cell phones didn't work. A fast trip to Campbell River, some 25 miles away, and back I guess.

Around 10pm we decide it's action time. It's been dark for 2 hours, and there are limited movements of inflatables across the water. We dress warmly, pinning our police shields in the center of our vests. We holster stun guns, take some handcuffs, and a lone GPS tracking device. One other device given to us at the last minute is a cell signal jammer. We presume the girls are using a cell phone as a hotspot for their computer link, since we saw no satellite dish attachments on the top archway in our earlier reconnaissance. We motor to within 100 yards of our target boat, and then cut the engine. Priscilla, the strongest of us, silently rows until we're under the bow of the Bayliner. Anna reaches up and places the GPS locator under the spot where the anchor chain falls freely from its channel. We paddle with our hands to the rear. The water is maybe 55 degrees or so, so not cold by any means.

There are three zodiacs fastened to the transom. As expected, each zodiac driver, fearing no encroachment, has left his key in the ignition. We confiscate them all, and tie up as silently as possible. Surprising us however, a light goes on in the inside cabin area, a door slides open, and a husky female voice yells, "Is there someone out here?" We hunker down, hoping the woman doesn't come outside to the back deck. We're lucky. We hear the door slide shut, and seconds later the light goes out. We whisper, wondering what we did that alarmed her. No idea. Best guess, somehow we rocked the boat with our arrival efforts. We jam the cell signals, climb over the transom and ease the back sliding door open. There are two male wind jackets thrown against the settees, and irregular strains of laughter floating up the companionway stairs. One of the jackets holds a wallet, easily removed. Sounds like activity behind closed doors in staterooms downstairs. We assume the boat has been modified to create three small staterooms instead of the standard two. Time for action.

We could be making a giant mistake. Maybe it's a family rendezvous, and guests have come by for a local get together. We each listen outside a stateroom door. Crude phrases emanate from behind the one I've chosen. Not consistent with a nice family reunion. I nod to Anna and Priscilla and we burst through the doorways in unison, stun guns in hand. The shouts responding to our intrusion vary in annoyance and intensity. "Get out." "Who are you?" "What the fuck?" "What's going on?" "You're trespassing." The pair I confront are busy bonking to the sounds of exertion and fake moans. All I see at first is a male butt and a shock of blonde hair on a pillow. Things get deflated in a hurry. I point to my police shield. "Police. Get dressed. You are both under arrest."

"What for?" the gal yells at me. "Prostitution," I answer. "Bullshit," she responds. "My friend Jack here and I are simply having a good time. Who the fuck are you on my boat? You don't look like police." As I turn to confront her more directly, Jack grabs his clothes and bolts for the doorway. Good try, but his hairy ass and back make an easy target for my gun and he goes down writhing across the doorstep. Over the years, regulations on the use of stun guns by authorities have given us lots more discretion. Jack probably doesn't know that.

The gal is still protesting. "Leave me alone. I've done nothing wrong. Get offa my boat." She doesn't even bother to cover up. Sassy miss. Blonde hair askew, black skin, smeared lipstick, large upright tits, shaved snatch, fingernails and toenails painted bright blue. I pick up some sort of gown off the floor and throw it to her. She reaches under the pillow and pulls out a smartphone. "Won't work," I tell her. "Stay in this cabin until I return." I pull Jack into the corridor, and slam the door shut.

Anna and Priscilla are leading two sorry-looking males into the downstairs lounge. They both are sporting flexible plastic link cuffs tying their hands behind them, but nothing else. One must be fifty years old, the other early twenties. Takes all types. I head to our zodiac, release the jamming mode, and call Ron quickly. I tell him I'll paint the target boat with a laser marker, so he can find it easily. He promises to hurry. I reset the jamming gear.

We gather all six party people and array them on the lounge settees. I warn them to be silent else we'll gag them. The three of us retire outside to the back deck and close the big glass sliding door through which we can see inside perfectly. We share our take-down stories, I'm the only one who needed to use my gun. The other two guys went quietly, the older one worrying because this wasn't the first time he'd been caught. We laugh at some of the antics the gals tried to pull, one even attempting a rape story.

Ron and Stuart and two other officers turn up forty minutes later, honing in on the laser target. We hand them the zodiac ignition keys, and wallet, dictate our findings into the recording device they brought, and take our leave, once again releasing the jamming mechanism.

A successful evening over, we head back to our stern-tie position, having promised the Campbell River officers that we'll check out Grace Harbour the following day.

Late morning we detour past the empty shell of the 4588 we'd raided last night, wondering what would become of it. Not our problem.   Grace Harbour is almost due south of Prideaux, across an extensive ridge of rocky terrain. The harbour is known for its alluring coves, twelve nautical miles away around Zephine Head leading into the Okeover Arm. As we're heading down the Arm we make a reservation at the Laughing Oyster, a top class restaurant on the east coast of the Malaspina Peninsula.

I'm thinking this will be a fun day, perhaps with no second brothel boat to tame. Sure enough, we search the whole harbour, SE to NW, twice, as well as Theodosia Arm, but no sign of a triangled quarry.   We wonder if there'll be disappointed clients tonight looking for an 'entertainment' venue.

I lay on the front deck pads, very relaxed, soaking up the lovely warm sunshine, and fall asleep. Two hours later, I awake to Anna's hand on my right breast. "Time for late lunch nourishment," she whispers. I let her lead me downstairs.

Odd Search

Classified/Homeland Security (map attached)

I look up as a shadow settles across the bow of our cruiser, replacing the sunlight on the front pads. 'Umbridge Delivery' stenciled across the machine's belly, 100 feet above us. Quiet bastards, they've really improved the technology over the last ten years. A slight hum is all I can detect, and I am concentrating hard even then. As expected, a small drone less than 2 feet across hones in on the front deck, a six inch cubic package in its grip talons. I notice the anti-slip pads that allow the package to be placed on the slight slope of the deck. Clever stuff.

Anna and Priscilla are leaning over two of the outboards, both with their top ends raised open. I shout to get the girls' attention. "Package arrival. Looks like another of your 'plain-brown wrapper' toys Anna. Can't you have them sent to your apartment, rather than here?" 'Here' was our deep-water dock space on the customs levy at Roche Harbor. It is a slow day, no threats anticipated, a gorgeous late summer blue-sky offering that has families and adult groups out for possibly one last gathering in warm waters.

Anna comes forward, brushing her red hair back from her forehead. "Well Kath, I like to show off the latest and greatest in capturing 'physique intelligence' as soon as I have access. This will be the new Q4 Reader announced just a week ago. The beauty of this is it simulates what a full readiness position might offer. In high def video no less."

She grabs the parcel, checks she is the intended recipient, and tears the wrappers off post haste. I look in amazement at the gadget she extracts. It has the form of an old fashioned watch you used to strap on your wrist. The skin-colored hold-clips these days of course have some sort of flexible biometric magnets that conform to anyone's wrist almost instantly. On the inside of the device there is a flat video screen possibly 1.5" by 1", and a single push button at one end. It can clearly be used very discreetly.

Priscilla is watching as Anna straps it on. I can tell she is dying to see it in action. She's been incredibly vocal about men's 'appointments', as she calls them, ever since I've known her, more than two years now. "It's not length," she'd say. "We only have 5 inches available. It's girth that matters gals. How filled we can be. You don't want something that doesn't touch the sides." Anna had hinted that this new machine – she called it a 'Statvibe' - would yield accurate measurements and projections of male genitals as long as the target was within 5 feet. The makers promised longer focal lengths, knowing the current version was somewhat limited in its usefulness.

Anna looks around. "Anyone we can invite on board to help with engine checks say, to test this out? Are Warren or David in the office Katherine?"

I hesitate. We three enjoy a little sexual fun at odd times, but it has to be tempered to not interfere with official duties.

"What's wrong with the engines?" I ask. Anna replies. "Nothing now. We had to clean some filters that's all. Our problem is that neither of us can reach back far enough to twist the last clamp into position. One drawback to having good-sized boobs. I'm not in for crushing my assets."

"OK. I'll see if Warren has a few minutes available. But for crying out loud Anna, be discreet. No outbursts till he's well on his way back to the office. OK?"

"Might be hard boss from the little I know about him already. Something about Aussie anatomy being more primitive than mere American physique. But go ahead, call him."

As I tap my throat nodule a strange warbling siren emanates from under the dashboard. Warren can hear it through the intercom. "Kath, sounds like a radiation alert. A bit odd out here in the sticks. Maybe a faulty indicator. We're not getting anything here in the office. Have you had any electronic malfunctions in the last couple of days?"

I hit a switch under the console, shutting down the warble and bringing up the chartplotter on the large video screen. A very faint yellow circle out near Sentinel Island fades in and out, clearly at the limits of our detection capabilities, if indeed they are working properly. I tell Warren what we can see and mention we have no electronic problems, although we could do with his help shutting down tops on two of the outboards. He promises to be right here, adding a suggestion that after his visit we might want to head out and patrol a wide berth near the Canadian border just in case someone is smuggling radioactive material.

Seems a far-fetched likelihood to me, but a ride out on the calm waters won't go astray, so we start getting ready for an exodus. It isn't long before the ordinary citizens ogling our boat part and Warren hops on board. Forty years old, handsome, with a shock of white hair, a day's growth around his chin and cheeks, aquiline nose, bright sparkling blue eyes. We all know his wife, Vicki, a beautiful specimen of the female race whom we all wish would join our 'club'. Oh yes.

"Hi ladies. What's the problem with the outboards?" Priscilla explains, as Anna maneuvers into position for a strategic vision capture with her new toy. She just has enough time before Warren turns and bends over the offending 200 hp monsters. His butt stretching tight in his white uniform slacks is sheer eye candy. A blatant pat would be too much, but I head back beside him, and manage a nice touch as I squeeze past to his starboard side. He grins. He knows what I am about. "There you go ladies. Try to keep it under 70 knots please. Have fun out there."

And he is gone, as quickly as he arrived. Curiosity killed the cat they say. Can't match what we three felines were about as we head down the three steps into the cuddy and out of the sunlight. The resolution on Anna's wrist image is remarkable. Warren's crown jewels are silhouetted in stark black and white. Perhaps a little larger than most men's of his age, but nothing like some late teenagers' offerings we'd all seen. "Pretty standard," I suggested.

"Yeah, but wait." It'll take a few seconds to bring up the 'aroused' projection images and measurements when I hit the switch. So don't be impatient."

I don't know how many millions of data points IBM must have analyzed in order to provide some small porn-data company the appropriate information for their algorithms, but the resultant image of a phallus at 6.5" length and 5.5" inches girth is definitely titillating. Hot stuff. Both measurements are deemed to be within the 95th percentile of comparative data. I believe it.

The image shuts down as Anna twists her wrist, and we stare at each other marveling at the advanced technology we've just seen in action. Of course - technology. More honestly, technology plus anatomy. Priscilla can't help herself. "See, now we know why Vicki has a permanent smile on her face. Lucky lady."

We head upstairs, and I start the engines idling, waiting for the girls to release the dock lines. While it is time to get serious, the sunshine and the sexual merriment have us all in a light mood. I head out past Spieden Island, wondering if we'll pick up the radiation detection warble again. We elect to head northwest towards Stuart Island and it's two partners, Johns and Satellite islands. Lots of boats out in all the bays.

Prevost Harbor is one of my favorites so we anchor there and take the inflatable to the park area on Stuart. Teenagers are having a ball jumping from the bridge that leads to the water dock where five or more families are enjoying a reunion with their boats jammed tightly against one another.

Born without the inhibitions that were in place twenty-five years ago, the teen gals wear only bikini bottoms, no tops, their nubile frames reminding each of us what we looked like ten years earlier. Some modesty is still a lingering part of our lives, and in a way we envy these free spirits who don't seem to care.

None of us have kids. None of us want kids. Perhaps one of the bonds that keeps us companionable. We have similar life-stories about dysfunctional families, and parents who faked love for each other. I wonder about the pairs of parents down on the docks and what their kids perceive about home life. How many will marry, how many will stay happily unshackled like the three of us?

Back at our 40 ft high-performance cruiser, we decide to head northeast, parallel to the Canadian border and check out Sucia Island State Park, with its highly popular coves. Shallow Bay and Fox Cove are surprisingly quiet. One of the entrance buoys at Shallow Bay is still broken. It drags underwater at high tide and is hard to see – a definite hazard. We radio our concerns to the park authorities. Fossil Bay and Snoring Bay are in shadow, harboring less than five boats total. We guess that Echo Bay to the north is where we'll find all the action.

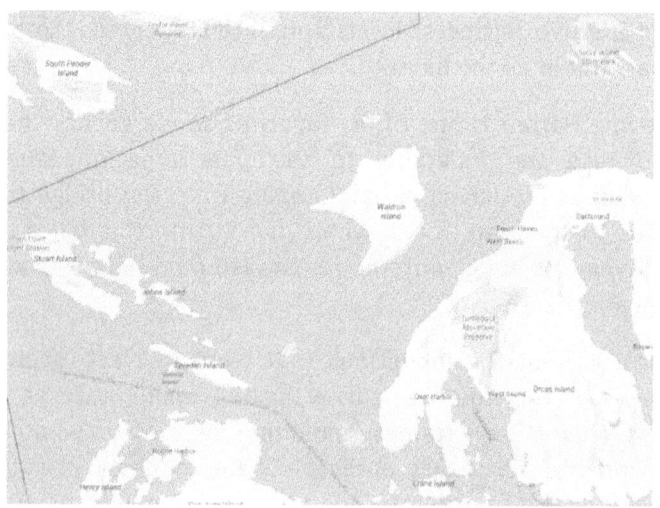

As we turn around Johnson Point the radiation warble starts up. It catches us by surprise as we'd basically forgotten about it, assuming some electronic anomaly in our system.

But here it is again. It fades out as we proceed northwest along the shores of South Finger Island, but the second we pass the yellow temporary mooring stand, it increases in velocity. I order Priscilla to notify headquarters and to connect to SkyLock. Warren, back at Roche, asks SkyLock for more details if possible. We have a solid yellow ring flashing strongly on the map over near the two Cluster Islands location.

I turn on our siren, and make a fast 135 degree starboard turn, throwing a large curved wake that irritates a number of boats anchored nearby. Sorry folks. Emergency. The wild rocking will stop, I promise. Warren is giving us information. "Doesn't look threatening ladies. Target is an old 35 foot Bertram flybridge. There's a couple sitting on the back deck, several young kids swimming nearby. That's as much as I can give you, sorry. Let us know what you find. Make sure your GeigSens battery handhelds are charged. And take care. Put on your personal shields before engaging further."

I signal Anna, who pulls out three multi-protection vests from a locker. As we slow down to come alongside the old yacht, we all don the bulky jackets. The yellow audible warning is at fever pitch, so I cut back its noise level. The couple on the boat look scared as we pull parallel. Who wouldn't? Out of the blue on a lazy summer afternoon this incredible hunk of sea-bound energy comes tearing across the water at high speed to engage you. Their reaction is understandable. Priscilla jumps over their boat's side railing, walks quickly to the back deck, and explains who we are, and how we've detected a radiation leak coming from their boat.

The woman sitting in a simple lawn chair hasn't taken her hand from her mouth since the minute she'd first spotted us charging flat out towards her. She is clearly in shock. I join Priscilla. "Sir, madam, we have to search your boat for the radiation source. Our concern is that it might be something planted on your boat by a third party. Are either of you feeling ill by chance? Headaches, nausea, unusual sea-sickness, fainting spells? Have any strangers asked you to carry a parcel for them?"

Both heads nod 'no', but that isn't enough. I send Priscilla onwards to check the downstairs cabins and the upper bridge, using the GeigSens unit, while I try further to calm the boat owners. "Where have you folks come from today?" Friday Harbor is the answer. The old chap has found his voice. "We thought it would be a nice day for the grandkids to go swimming here. Can they come aboard? They're all behind you now in the water by the dive platform." I shake my head. "Sorry, not till we find the radiation source. Please urge them to stay calm."

Priscilla emerges through the saloon sliding door. "Got it boss. Source is in the small back cabin, reading 'unknown type' but 'secure level'. There's a chap sleeping down there and I didn't dare wake him. But it's clear he's the source. The counter registers strongest in the lower part of his body. Looks like our vests aren't needed though."

"Oh, that's our son Tim, father of all these urchins," Grandma pipes up. "His wife's a nurse and had to work today so we came out without her."

I tell Priscilla to go wake the man gently, and bring him outdoors. I turn back to Grandma and Grandpa. "Where does Tim work? Has he been in any strange places recently? Has he been sick? Any place he could have been exposed to radiation?" I have to explore this thoroughly.

Just as Tim and Priscilla emerge, Grandpa jumps up "I've got it! It's why Tim is sleeping. Just yesterday he had radiation seeding for prostate cancer. Son, do you have that card the oncologist gave you?"

Poor Tim is out of it. "Huh. What?" are his only intelligible responses. One of the late teen boys clinging to the transom speaks up. "I know where it is. Can I get it?" I think at that moment all of us breathe a huge sigh of relief. I signal Anna to shut down the siren and to let Warren know what we've learned. We scan the card the young chap brings us, sending its image back to headquarters, from where it is passed on to the health authorities.

In fifteen minutes we receive an 'all-clear' signal, and we prepare to depart. There are twenty zodiacs in our vicinity belonging to curious visitors. Anna yells at them to back off. We apologize to the family for our intrusion. Grandpa is smiling. "That's OK, most excitement we've had in years. Too bad Tim won't remember much about it." I wish them a happy remainder of the afternoon, ask that our best wishes for cancer control be passed to Tim when he re-awakes.

We pull away and slowly head back to our home port. Enough excitement for one day. Anna is deep in thought for most of the trip but as we round Spieden Island she speaks up. "Guess that's one cancer we gals don't have to worry about. Wonder if my new device would have detected those radiation seeds and what their half-life is. Might do some research tonight. Either of you care to join me?"

"Sure thing," Priscilla responds. What do you think the Statvibe might say about a female toy?"

Massive Catch

Table of Contents

Chapter 1. As it is, as it was. The Year 2050

<u>The most relevant societal, technological, and government matters affecting the U.S. are as follows:</u>

- IT implants and wearables are an everyday phenomenon

- Police have a nationwide department under Homeland Security. There is much flexibility for law enforcement officers in the use of non-lethal weapons

- Lots more drones of varying types exist – from military to personal, including home delivery, high def video doctor assessment and services, urgent medicine needs, building inspection

- Major female liberation. There are far more women than men these days in management ranks across all professional aspects of society. Women rule. An interesting consequence is that people of both sexes talk about sex more openly in the workplace. The definition of sexual harassment has changed to require far more intense episodes.

- Internet porn sites are forced to use a specific extension, and porn is diminishing in production and usage.

- Early on, the U.S. government dramatically changed the welfare and healthcare system. Medical research was significantly enhanced, and now, everyone gets access to good health care free. Welfare out-payments have become more efficient. There are better incentives to work, and limited support for those who have kids and stay at home.

- Incompetent mayors in rife torn cities were thrown out, and gradually a new sense of order became established.

Riots were minimized, lines of racial inequality began to blur, and women became more important sources of change. Higher penalties for deadly gun use were passed, and guns became much harder to obtain. A tax on hospital childbirth was imposed, the message being it's a serious business to have a child. Similarly, there is a heavy tax to become an immigrant.

Changes that are more global and their U.S. implications

- The U.S. has stopped financing the U.N., and being the prominent watchdog for democracy in third and fourth world nations. The country spends heavily on defense and security. The rest of the world regrets the U.S. action and is struggling with a response.

- Thirty plus years back, a new path started to be forged in many parts of the world. Isolationism, parochialism, anti-globalism began to emerge on a wider scale. A U.S. president with limited time in office started it by building a defensive combination fence and wall all the way across the southern border. European countries beset by middle eastern refugees followed suit. The U.S./Mexico barrier, dramatically cut the transfer northwards of drugs and illegal aliens. Drug flow from Central America switched to submarines travelling to Canada, then any means to cross the border into the U.S.

- Canada almost acts like an appended U.S. state. The country has cut back on defense, rides on U.S. defense coat tails and gives the U.S. almost open access to local immigration control.

- Over 6 million criminals from Mexico and Central America have been deported since 2017. A controlled immigration state was put in place with credentialed workers and students encouraged to enter. At the same time, port border entrances were closed to all religious zealots and citizens of certain middle eastern countries, and the pursuit of jihadist terrorists was upgraded to the highest priority. Schools teaching Sharia law were closed down and thousands of non-productive members of religious sects deported. Those immigrants allowed in to the U.S. today are forced to have a sensor chip implanted under their skin near a shoulder.

- A sense of pride has started to return in various societies, and a willingness to live without owning everything. There are emerging national causes that promote and reward craftsmanship and other aspects of the arts, unseen for nearly thirty years. A renewed interest in literature has returned words like beauty, craftsmanship, honesty and integrity into the language of reporters, pundits and analysts. The media industry has experienced major consolidation as sensationalism and bias has been overtaken by truth, fairness, and objectiveness in journalistic reporting. The industrial scene has changed markedly. Heavy industries are required to be totally non-polluting. While technology still advances, things like watches and cameras have disappeared. Gadgets enhancing human efficiency, transportation, and food production are a way of life.

- A long-lost word, 'statesmanship', has re-emerged in expert commentary as world leaders show more concern for their countries than their personal positions. Communication is more civil, and while there is an

increased number of political parties now in many countries, the general political tone has changed. Parties seem to be helping each other do the best for constituents by enhancing other parties' programs and initiatives. Medical improvements have had an incredible effect on treatment of the most debilitating diseases. No female born in the last fifteen years at an accredited hospital need ever experience menstruation, no male will die of prostate cancer, and few women will suffer breast cancer. Births can be programmed to the day if desired.

- Yet, even with all the positive programs, activities, and improved life outlooks, there are still those unhappy with their lot. The main problem area in many countries is still with drugs. Of course these days the primary problem is with synthetic drugs, as world-wide programs to eradicate naturally occurring drug plants have almost killed the corresponding threats. And the sources have changed. Sophisticated chemical labs in Central America and in Europe manufacture potent new synthetic drugs in wide ranging variety. And, unfortunately there are always buyers ready to generate a new high for themselves. These folks just don't seem to understand, or perhaps care about, the consequences of a state of 'addiction'.

Above summary for perspective only. Views may change over time. Not to be quoted without permission.

An example of some of the changes noted above follows in the attached incident report.

Chapter 2. Homeland Security Archive. Report NW-I9-4579

Classified/Homeland Security (map attached)

I inch the boat's throttle back to idle, and the heavily modified Mercs ease down from a wide open ear-shattering roar to a whimpering 50 decibels. Conversation level. The vessel gradually settles and I turn to my two partners, Anna and Priscilla. I relay the transcribed text message I've just received deep in my inner ear, courtesy of the implant there. "We're on standby. About to receive a download with new information from one of the SkyLocks located somewhere over Sidney."

Sidney is a small town on the Saanich peninsula at the eastern end of Vancouver Island, Canada. Our team has been there many times. Friendly retirement community, close to Victoria airport, Butchart Gardens, and Swartz Bay. The huge British Columbia Car Ferries in their stately white and blue livery depart from the Swartz regularly for Tsawwassen on the mainland. They're graceful in their stable ride through the islands, a contrast to the iconic green and cream Washington state car ferries that dock directly at Sidney, 4 miles south, instead. For tourist-owned sail and motor boats, Sidney offers one of the peninsula's prettier and better managed marinas with its dockside hanging baskets in Spring through Fall. It provides a well-used Canadian Customs port of entry for U.S. boats heading into the Canadian Gulf Islands.

The unusual halt to our assignment suggests a major change in activity coming up. I chafe metaphorically since we had just made visual contact with a potential smuggler's speedboat hauling ass southeast down the

Strait of Georgia. He was still 1000 yards off but Priscilla found him using her Swarovski range finding binocs. She has incredibly steady hands and 20/15 vision.

I wonder how long the download from the security satellite will take. Maybe if it's a short burst we'll be able to resume our operation.

Just as I finish the thought I get another message. 'Download abort. Technical difficulties. Retry one hour. Continue current mission.' It's as if headquarters has read my mind. Makes me pause. Is it possible that the chip in my head has functions beyond what I've been told? Guess I'll worry about that later. Right now it's back to active operation. I tell the girls. They grin. We all love our job.

We are three 23-27 year olds serving the country through Homeland Security in the U.S./Canadian border waters. Miscellaneous sea duties. Have a very fast outboard-driven intercept boat under our command. Each top of the line in our respective classes of recruits, we have been together nearly a year. All excellent swimmers, shooters, and martial arts proponents. Usually with an added element, called 'female surprise' when we apprehend terrorists, smugglers, drunken boat drivers and worse.

Today we're on drug interception maneuvers, watching for traffickers bringing death-by-powder into the U.S. from Canada. Canada? Oh yes, things have changed markedly since that massive wall was built along the southern U.S. border 30 plus years ago. There's still high demand for drugs in the U.S. But coordinated world-wide action has essentially eradicated 95% of the fields of natural stimulant plants in Central and Southern America. Today it's all about synthetic drugs. Well-paid scientists in isolated labs in small Central American towns, churn out highly complex, potentially lethal, combinations of chemicals that permanently impair the stupid and unwary.

The drug mafia now use submarines to deliver the manufactured killing substances to various Canadian ports. From there it's moved by plane, train, trucks or boats to the U.S. The rewards from street sale are enormous and the human delivery teams crossing the border vary from unsuspecting innocent tourists to ruthless criminals.

Our job is risky, and as dangerous as the drugs themselves. We three agents carry both high magnum pistols as well as stun guns, there being new regulations approving wide-ranging use of the latter. We have other powerful technology at our disposal as well. It includes high definition video streaming from SkyLock satellites and drones, rocket firing guns mounted fore and aft on our boat to take out engines on fleeing suspects, and fast tracking GPS transponders. As well, we carry cell and VHS

signal jamming equipment, gender confirming / personal search X-ray hand-concealed units, electronic probes to locate suspect powder or gel on selected target boats, and four small prowler camera drones capable of staying aloft noiselessly for two hours at 1000 feet. Who knows what we might need in any situation?

Back to reality. We are idling in our 40ft cruiser just west of Blaine, U.S. Washington State. We can see the Peace Arch at the U.S. / Canadian border and the large local marina that offers both permanent and visitor moorage. I switch off the geo-fence lock and turn so we are pointed 90 degrees to the course the fast speedboat is on. He's running at over 50 mph according to our radar information and will flash across our bow way ahead in less than a minute. I'm not sure even with our five Merc 200 outboards at full power that I'll be able to intercept the guy. But so saying, I yell "Hang on ladies," and cram the throttles forward. The engines scream, the bow lifts as the props change their grip in the water, and we jerk forward, up on plane in 10 seconds, speeding southwest towards the invisible border in the Strait of Georgia. Anna whoops with delight.

Priscilla identifies the suspect boat as a Cobalt R35, the shiny blue gelcoat making it look new. We're 90 yards to its left as it cuts across our vision heading for the border between Tumbo and Patos islands. Anna hits the sirens and flashers and the boat's driver turns his face towards us, but doesn't slow down. We're aware of most of the locally popular boat brands, and Cobalt is no exception.

 The R35 has 4 engine options in both the Volvo and Merc configurations. This boat must be fitted with one of the most powerful versions.

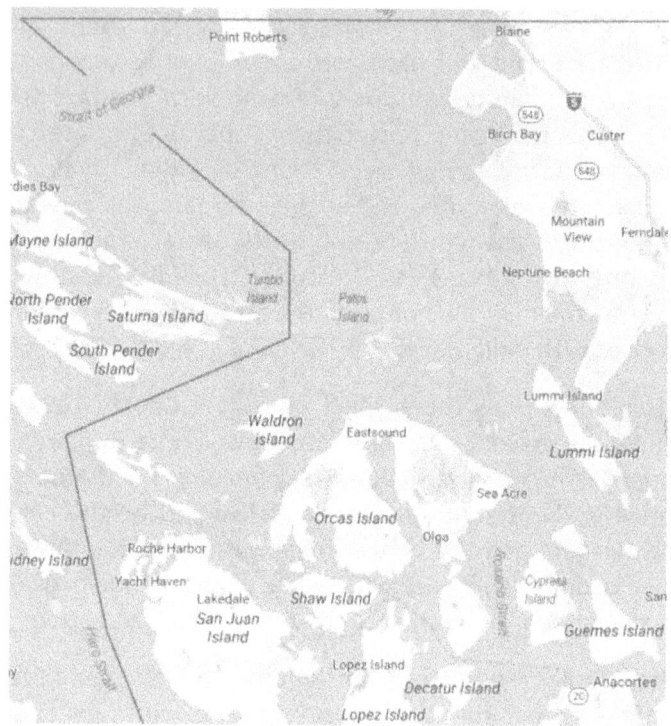

The driver scares us on two counts. There are other pleasure boats out on the waters and his speed is a danger to them. And if he is smuggling dope he's a scary dude in his own right. I jam the throttles to their max position but we can't quite match his speed. The rooster tail from his back end is 10 feet tall and his wake is strong enough to form decent 18 inch-high waves.

We turn, 100 or so yards in arrears and steer into the clear spot in the middle of his wake. With our heads together to offset the noise of the outboards, we conclude he must be heading for Anacortes unless he's going to make a run along Whidbey Island and into Puget Sound. He slows down a little to turn around the northeastern point of Orcas Island and head south into Rosario Strait.

We wonder. What on earth is he smuggling and what is his destination?

Chapter 3. Chase and intercept

I smile. This is where I excel. I know my blood pressure is probably ramping up but I actually feel icy calm and controlled. Unlike our target, I don't slow down an iota, but pull a 2G starboard turn, the pros on the two port engines lifting above the surface and screaming their dislike. Anna and Priscilla hang on tightly. When we settle back on equilibrium I'm only 85 yards behind. We watch intently. Will he turn left around Cypress Island and head through the Guemes Channel to Anacortes, or continue due south?

We've guessed right. The Cobalt slows again, but not enough in our view. The driver makes a terrible left turn, coming within 25 yards of one of the large car-carrying ferries that is heading for the Anacortes docks. His wake washes against the big boat, splashing passengers at the railing, who recoil, surprised and scared. We watch with our hearts in our mouths as the Cobalt driver recovers control just in time to avert a horrible disaster. To come that close is not only a very big no no, but also incredibly frightening. Those ferries are heavy, resilient vessels, and when steaming at 20 knots with a full load of passengers and vehicles, not something to tangle with. Well-intentioned sea safety rules require other boats to stay at least 100 yards away from the ferries.

The Cobalt driver must have been scared out of his wits as the ferry suddenly loomed in his face and filled his entire vision. We don't understand how he couldn't have been watching.

The ferry captain slows his ship down and sends out five powerful blasts on his horn, no doubt taking appropriate photos of the near collision in support of an immediate radio call to the authorities. We wave to the captain on the bridge indicating we'll manage the situation. We get an appreciative wave back.

As a result of the Cobalt driver's miscalculation we are now within 40 yards of his boat, no doubt providing visual thrills galore for many of the passengers on the ferry and folks in other close-by pleasure boats. As the Cobalt veers away to safety the driver suddenly cuts his speed totally and drifts slowly to a stop. We pull alongside, turn off the sirens, but leave the lights flashing so other boats see us and stay clear.

The driver has crumpled in the captain's chair and a companion is bending over him. We tie our boat to the Cobalt fore and aft, I get out the drug probes, and we all jump on board the interloper. I announce who we are, but there's no response. Anna moves forward and pulls a heavy-set man back from his position by the driver. She passes him back to Priscilla who pushes him down roughly on the rear cabin seats. He starts to talk, but Priscilla shushes him.

The scene at the Captain's chair is ugly. The driver is no older than twenty. He's puked over the control panel and the floor in front of his seat, and has soiled his pants. The air smells gross around him. He rests his head on his arms across the steering wheel. He's shaking from the shock of narrowly averting a terrible crash with the ferry. Anna pulls his head up by his hair. The kid's face is pale and his eyes are glazed. He mumbles incoherently, and Anna drops his head back down. "Stoned," she mutters. Explains a lot.

I head towards the chap slumped on the back seat. I think he may be recovering from shock. I can imagine how suddenly having the shadow of a giant ferry in your face would have that effect. Nevertheless, I explain our interest in checking the craft for safety features, and show him my credentials. By the look on his face I can tell he knows the reasoning is farcical. He dutifully complains about our harassment, and the unnecessary stoppage, since their boat is new. I tell Priscilla to search the storage compartments in the cockpit area to see what we might find. Frankly however, I expect any drugs will be concealed downstairs in the cabin or head. I give her one of the close-distance sensitive probes.

There's an accent in the chap's voice that is bothering me. Most drug runners we encounter are either Canadian or Central American. This accent is more middle eastern, and he has the dark, swarthy looks of someone from that part of the world. What is going on?
"Leave the kid alone, but grab the ignition keys" I tell Anna. "Then search downstairs for a stash." I give her the other probe. Maybe the kid is high on whatever he's smuggling. Anna reaches across him and removes the keys, dropping them in her pants pocket. The man Priscilla and I are guarding yells "Our property! Give back." Priscilla looks at him with disdain, and says "When we're done, shitface. Passports?"

The chap's face clouds over. I figure he's looking for a fight. He's a bull of a man. Over six feet tall, broad shoulders, chest like a barrel, black hair brushed forward and upwards. Physique of a weight-lifter. His expression changes into a threatening scowl.

He surprises all of us by suddenly squeezing by Priscilla and leaping from his boat to ours, probably intent on breaking something aboard. Quick on the draw Pricilla hits him in the back of his left leg with a bolt from her stun gun. He falls and Priscilla prepares to follow and secure him.

The phaser must not have been at full force however, for he groans and immediately stands up. His stamina is evident, for he lunges forward to attack Priscilla as she jumps onto one of the rubber fenders. Mistake. She's seen his move and grabs for the high cabin outdoor handrail with both hands, swinging her feet in a sharp upward curve and burying her boots in his abdomen. He doubles over and screams in a foreign language. He stumbles backward further into the cockpit area. At which point Priscilla moves in. She pivots on one leg, twirls 180 degrees and with a perfect martial arts maneuver crunches her right foot against the side of the chap's face. As he starts to wobble, she drives full force blows with the heels of her open hands against both his ears. He's almost out from the resultant pain but as he finally subsides to the deck floor she delivers the coup de grace – a massive kick to his groin. She jumps on him, turns him over, pulls his arms behind him and cuffs him with the new electronic grips. He starts whimpering, at which point she jams a mouth lock between his teeth where it clamps on to both his lips and teeth, and silences him.

Breathing heavily, she turns towards Anna and me on the Cobalt, raises the thumb on her right hand and yells "All secure boss."

I hope she's right, as something still doesn't add up correctly in my mind.

Chapter 4. A real find

We've been distracted watching Priscilla and suddenly are caught unawares. A thick hairy arm reaches out through the open companionway door from the cuddy cabin and violently pulls Anna by the neck of her uniform across the threshold into the cabin below. She hits her head on a step and I hear her moan. The barrel of a black pistol is poked forward, aimed directly at me.

I duck behind the driver's seat, wary of the gunman's intent. Does he plan to use Anna as a hostage, or is he going to shoot his way out with her as his shield? In the instant I deliberate there is a sizzling 'zap' sound and the gunman's pistol goes flying, his fingers dangling uselessly. Markswoman Priscilla to the rescue. I jump forward and apply a headlock to the antagonist and pull him over Anna's body out of the companionway. He reaches up with his good hand, grabs my hair and yanks. "Yow." My head jerks back but I refuse to give up my grip. Next thing I know Priscilla has returned and delivers a hard hand edge karate chop to the man's throat and he goes limp.

We bind the guy into immobility and gag him with a mouthpiece. Priscilla picks him up then drops him like a sack of potatoes on the rear cabin seat. His very existence, hidden in the cuddy cabin, makes us think we may have captured a terrorist, rather than a bunch of drug runners.

I attend to Anna who is struggling to regain a sense of reality. Priscilla pulls the driver from his stinking chair and dumps him next to his friend on the back seat. He offers no resistance.

Anna is upside down on the three steps going down to the cuddy, her head on the galley floor, her legs stretching up and out thru the companionway to the cockpit floor. I squeeze down beside her and lift her head gently. I feel a large bump at the back. She smiles at me "Did you get him?" I nod 'yes'. She must have been knocked unconscious to have to ask. I help her slide down and assume a sitting position. There's an empty unused glass in a cabinet above the sink so I offer her some water, which she drinks slowly. A little color is already returning to her cheeks. Priscilla comes to the open doorway, her eyebrows raised in question. "She'll be OK," I offer. "Contact Donna at HQ, and catch her up on things."

Donna Campbell is my immediate boss, located in Roche Harbor on San Juan Island. There are far more women than men these days in the manager ranks of our division of Homeland Security. Actually that's true in education, religion, politics, systems technology, heavy industry, and government. No looking up skirts through glass ceilings. Women have advanced well beyond women's lib and their traditional matriarchal roles in the last thirty years.

Anna is recovering fast. She waves the probe around and says "I'll be fine Kath. Go talk to Donna while I check the staterooms out." I poke my head upstairs and see Priscilla is back on our boat. She taps the personal communication nodule in her throat and points the Electronic Communication Module or ECM at the big screen. A few seconds later Donna's image lights up the left half of the screen, the right showing an image from above of our cruiser tied to the Cobalt.

Priscilla explains how we chased what we thought was a smuggling suspect, but have in custody at least one, maybe two terrorists. Down below I find three passports next to the water glasses. I head onto our cruiser and wave my wrist image device across each passport in turn, a copy appearing on the large screen. Two of the diplomatic booklets are in Arabic, one is Canadian.

Donna speaks up. "We intercepted the emergency call the ferry captain made, and refocused a SkyLock drone to the GPS location.   Good work collaring those pricks. How's Anna?"

"Needs a headache pill, and an all-purpose medic heal-package for a bump on the back of her head, but otherwise OK. Priscilla is heading back to check on her."

"Well, we have a land-based unit from the Anacortes office on its way to you. Let's see. Yep – their zodiac is 250 yards away so will be with you momentarily. They can take the three prisoners and the Cobalt and do the interrogation and arrange charges etc. Can you turn your flashers off? They're interfering a bit with your image at this end. And I see from your control panel that you used

 a lot of gas in your chase. I suggest you refuel, then go anchor in a safe spot and rest up for a bit. But stay in touch. There's another development under way."

As the local land team pulls into view, Donna signs off. We hand over the three men, together with their passports and the ignition keys. One of the officers immediately assumes guard with a very menacing assault rifle pointing at the interlopers. We attach a 75 foot tow rope between the zodiac and the Cobalt, unravel the lines holding us together and push the Cobalt away.

I high-five the girls, and we head for the nearest marina that offers fuel.

Chapter 5. Respite

All three of us feel drained. Good reason. Usually our intercepts don't become so physical. I'm the least affected, but the three of us have become very close and I feel for my companions emotionally. "You two are awesome," I tell them for the umpteenth time. "And I know just the place for us to go hangout."

We head west to Spencer Spit, a small peninsula sandbar relatively unfamiliar to most local boaters. We anchor within 50 yards of the beach, not another vessel in sight. Just what we need – privacy. The sun is warm, so we retrieve our bathing suits stored in a back locker. That is, Anna and I put our bikini bottoms on and head for the big mat on the bow deck. With the new age of greater sexual liberty, teen girls and young women like us go top-free, even though our three figures are not as nubile as they once were. Priscilla wants an overall tan and heads for the back deck, au naturel. She's sporting a new landing strip. Two parallel well-defined hair lines perhaps an inch or so apart. I compliment her, and she tells me it's in response to a male friend's request. Lucky man. Bet he loves her 36D golden orbs as well. Ah, to be bi.

We all doze off, but are awakened by raucous male 'yahoos' and wolf whistles about an hour later. A small flybridge yacht is quietly idling no more than fifteen yards off our port side and several guys are enjoying the views we provide. I press the band around my left wrist and our sirens and flashers are immediately activated. The guys take off like a rocket, probably wondering if we'll chase them and pull them over. We have no interest.

We three, individually and jointly, enjoy a little sexual fun at odd times, but we temper it and make sure it doesn't interfere with official duties. It is nice to know however that our bodies are still attractive to the opposite sex, even though some of us aren't interested in engaging physically with its members these days. Lots of related common interests. For example, none of us have kids. None of us want kids. Perhaps one of the bonds that keeps us companionable. We have similar life-stories about dysfunctional families, and parents who faked love for each other.

Our rest period disturbed, we change back into uniforms with some reluctance, and grab snacks from our kitbags. We sit by the outboards going over the morning's events, wondering what the land crew in Anacortes has discovered. What sort of terrorists did we apprehend? Where did they come from? Where were they headed? Did they intend to set up another training camp, or to develop and set off life-destroying bombs in crowded places? For years now port border entrances have been closed to all Muslims and Syrians, and pursuit of jihadist terrorists is backed by unlimited defense expenditure. The old Muslim schools teaching Sharia law are all closed down and thousands of non-productive religious zealots have been deported. Any immigrant allowed to stay in the U.S. these days is trackable through forced chip

implantation. We doubt our three captives will ever have that honor. More likely, they will be housed where they'll never see daylight again. The hundreds of new underground prisons across the extended badlands offer none. The only good thing about them is that they are a long way from any natural fault lines. Which means of course that those ensconced will enjoy their shelters for as long as they live.

The judicial system rarely focuses on prisoners once underground.

It's sort of ironic that by location the prisoners will survive forever, whereas the major quake along the western seaboard of the U.S. 5 years ago wiped out a lot of northern California towns, and two million innocent citizens. Torrential rains and hurricanes on the east coast had a similar effect, 10 years earlier. There are those who advocate building the next set of prisons near the fault lines, but research has shown it will be hard to find employees to manage them. The latest proposals tout an option of establishing prisoner colonies on the moon. Sort of akin to the Brits establishing Botany Bay In Australia as a prisoner colony 250 years ago.

I'm jolted out of my mindless wanderings by another text-interpreted signal deep in my eardrum. I pass on the news. "Five minutes max ladies before we move on. Told to expect a major download before that. Drug intercept task coming up. Anna, want to check that far port outboard engine? Sounded a little rough to me as we pulled up here. And Priscilla, double check comms

with HQ back at Roche. It's all too damned quiet sitting here doing nothing."

Anna reports. "Loose carb connection boss. Sound better now?" I turn sideways, listen for a few seconds as the engine idles, and nod. "Good job. Thanks."

On cue, Priscilla updates us. "Everything electronic in working order Kath. Ha, that reminds me of that old Scottish joke. What's worn under a man's kilt? Nothing, it's all in working order." I blow a raspberry letting her know what I think of her joke. Simultaneously I wonder how many kilts she might have checked under in her younger days. She'd toured Scotland as a late teenager. Bragged about how easy it was to create tilts in kilts among traditional sex-deprived male youths there. Still talks about returning.

A piercing alarm emanates from under the dash. It brings the three of us to full alert. The video screen flashes on and off then steadies and shows a picture of a sixty- or seventy-foot yacht at a long pier labelled Nanaimo Yacht Club H Dock. I choke back an exclamation – are we being shown a smuggler's yacht? Docked at a prestigious Yacht Club? Unbelievable what we are facing these days.

The video stream must be from a drone directly overhead, as the resolution is superb. I see a woman using a dolly to transport a stack of boxes to the boat. She stops at the rear deck and hands the boxes one by one over the railing. The upper deck overhang prevents

me seeing the recipient. Amazing that they are loading in broad daylight. I use my hand-held sensor to zoom in on the two remaining boxes on the dolly. Beer!

But something is off. The woman can hardly lift the second last box, very nearly depositing it in the dark water between the dock and the boat. More than beer I warrant. A man scurries off the back deck and picks up the last box, pushing the woman out of the way. She resists, so he gets in her face and she backs off. I know where my guess would focus for one source of contraband material.

Donna Campbell's face shows on the screen. What is this with Scots today? Her voice is commanding. "You're looking at a U.S. licensed 70 foot Azimut, named 'Sea-Thong'. Hardly an appropriate name. She's not skimpy in any way." The vessel is a modern Italian designed flybridge, with that characteristic swept-back look and large cabin windows almost down to the waterline. Awesome for sure.

I step closer to the video screen, but at that instant it starts pixelating and we lose the picture altogether. What on earth is going on? Has someone intercepted our comms link? This is highly unusual.

Chapter 6. No expense spared

Audio is still working, as a few seconds later Donna's voice comes through. "These creeps have some new jamming technology that our tech boys are studying. We can get satellite shots sometimes but as soon as we start increasing the resolution through drone cameras we run into problems. Apparently that shot at the dock is our first hint of a technology breakthrough, but clearly we have a long way to go. You should be seeing the satellite shot now on your screen. You can see the boat outline well enough but no detail." Her voice starts to fade. Last we hear is "I'll fill you in as best I can. We've been onto these guys for the last two days"

*   *   *

"Whoops. Dear visitor, your VR went black, right, but is now live again? I apologize for that. It indicates government censorship. Whatever vault or library you got this archived security episode from, I guess the authorities don't want you to know everything about our latest sky surveillance technology. I hope you were aware that there might be censorship along the way.

"A lot of viewers aren't. They think censorship only applies to Internet smut stuff.   Frankly, ever since the great liberation of women twenty plus years ago, porn has receded in intensity. Two reasons. Today sexual openness is so much more accepted, and porn sites are forced to use the url extension 'dot sex'. No longer ubiquitous, but limited in presence, and policed harder.

"By the way, while we wait to sync up with the record, let me ask, how do you like my avatar that is presenting this report? It's new, a customized version I created. The uniform is pretty exact and my face is close to real. I enhanced my figure a little by adding an inch or so up top and losing the same amount around the waist and hips. Anna adjusted her figure also, but Priscilla's avatar is as real as they come. Amazing how easy it is to use the new design software these days."

*   *   *

"OK, dear visitor, everything should be back to where it was before the blackout.   Let me reframe and link to our terrorist and smugglers' venture record."   I pause a few seconds to allow a real-time reset. Nanaimo, where the smugglers' boat is docked, is about 65 nautical miles from where we are, west of Anacortes. I wait for Donna at Roche Harbor o speak up again and formally send us northward across the border on a new quest. I signal Anna and Priscilla to be ready.

Right on cue, Donna comes through. "Ok ladies, gird your loins, we have a true nasty in our faces. This must be one of the biggest hauls ever attempted to cross the border. Stand by while I tell you what I know.

"Our best guess is that the vessel you were looking at will be transporting contraband from three submarine loads."

Anna interrupts. "Excuse me Donna, but I just don't understand. Why don't the Canucks intercept the subs as they arrive? It must take a bunch of men and women to move all the packages from boat to land. Aren't the folks up north watching for large unskilled labor gatherings?"

"I get as frustrated as you, Anna," Donna replies. "From what I gather, the smuggler groups use new encrypted cell communication, and the authorities usually only find out afterwards when a drunk member talks too much in a local pub. We benefit a bit, but not the talker. Loose talk often gets the speaker killed, his tongue cut out to make the reason obvious."

Priscilla grimaces. "Should be a warning to participants when the news gets around. Guess alcohol dulls some memories faster than others."

Donna continues. "As the price of drugs continues to sky-rocket, these groups can afford to become more sophisticated with technology, and more ruthless with respect to group membership. And their subs are small enough to pull into fairly shallow waters, so they can enter any number of small coves in the dead of night. There's no way that the authorities can cover them all."

Brainy Anna has her own ideas. "Maybe our research teams need to change their focus and work on detecting the submarines before they offload their killer cargoes. I know it's a wide ocean but can't they do more to police the waters around the northwest end of Vancouver Island?"

"Sounds easy, but just like our latest jet fighters, their subs are constantly deploying new stealth options which they hide behind. Wouldn't surprise me if that's what they have operating on this expensive vessel they call *Sea-Thong*. Who knows? As you can see we no longer have an image of the boat — they've activated some new electronic jamming function which our best and brightest haven't decoded yet."

I'm getting tired of the conversation and sitting around doing nothing, so I jump in. "OK Donna, what's our next steps? We're idling outside Anacortes, ready for action."

"Yeah, I know, don't get testy. We think this boat will be moving soon. Maybe you could head slowly towards Sidney and hang around at the marina. By the way, the two older chaps on the Cobalt you pulled over were both near the top of our anti-terrorist team's wanted list. Radical jihadists from Syria. Aren't faring well from the medical serum treatment apparently. And the stupid young driver is already in a cramped plastic transport cell on one of the cross-border immigration trucks. He'll be dumped at the Canadian transfer center for detention and assessment. Obviously of no real interest to our people.

"You done good ladies. Our security boys are very happy with your efforts." Her smile fills the screen.

Priscilla is the eldest of our trio. Largest in overall stature at 6ft 1in, with wide shoulders, she runs like a hare, is a crack shot, martial arts expert, and dead-lifts more than Anna and I can. And she's pretty, with wonderful interpersonal skills when needed, but icily serious when dealing with the sort of vermin we chase. She's a natural brownette, with thick lips, and high cheeks, hair cut shoulder length and bleached blonde. Physically attractive to both sexes. She and I have been lovers for a year now. She's a doll.

Anna is a couple of inches shorter, incredibly fit, agile as a monkey, swims like a fish, keen as they come. Cute, pixie face. Just twenty-three years old. Has fiery red hair masking an amazing intellect. I love her enthusiasm and zest for her job. Only been with us a short time. Not sure of her sexuality yet, hoping to learn her preferences soon. She's an absolute delight to have on the team.

As for me, I'm 26 years old, been in the job 4 years. This is my third team in that time, but without a doubt, the best. I'm not quite as good looking as my partners but still appealing, especially to the menfolk. Over time have had relationships with several of them. But now prefer my own kind. Gentler, sexier, more understanding. I'm the same height as Anna, but have tight curly hair, which is a pain to look after, but helps keep me looking unique. And while I hate to admit it I probably weigh a few pounds more than the other two. I have more experience than either of them, although they are both very fast learners.

Both of them have leadership potential. Just a matter of time till they have their own teams.

Chapter 7. Movement

We head south in Lopez Sound, easing by Rim Island, then out through Lopez Pass into the Salish Sea and Rosario Strait.

South of Lopez and San Juan islands we pick up a bit of chop from the winds coming down the Strait of Juan de Fuca, but not enough to bother us. It's getting late in the afternoon so the breeze has a definite bite to it, but even that disappears as we head north up Haro Strait.

We decide to have dinner at the restaurant named Haro's in the Sidney Pier Hotel & Spa by the marina. It's a bit of a splurge for each of us, but the food is delicious. We ask the restaurant manager where 'Haro' comes from. Turns out the Strait was named in 1790 by the commander of a Spanish ship in honor of the ship's pilot, Gonzalo López de Haro. Right. Nothing meaningful to any of us, and while our curiosity is quelled, we realize it's one of those odd pieces of information that we'll forget immediately. Seeing our looks of disappointment that the name wasn't more meaningful, the manager adds that Captain George Vancouver was the first to explore and map the Strait in detail in 1792. We agree that that fact we probably will remember.

Dusk is starting to settle, pink colored clouds high in the western sky. We head for the path along the foreshore, but all pause at the same time as our inner ear devices come alive with a not-to-be-ignored synthesized alert. The message is simple. 'Urgent, contact HQ. Repeat, urgent, contact HQ.'

Highly meaningful if such a signal is sent to all three of us, usually it would come to me alone. I touch my throat nodule. Donna's voice comes through loud and clear. "Looks like the smugglers are on the move Kath. Are you on your boat?"

"No, but we can be in 5 minutes."

"Then go. Call me when you have a map up on your screen. We want to nail these guys. Out."

I motion to the girls that we have to move, and we start jogging back to the marina. Bystanders stare as we up the pace and run along the piers to our vessel. I start the engines, Anna unties us, and Priscilla sets up the comms. I back out of the finger slip carefully, and steer for the outer breakwater defining the exit channel.   Clear of the marina I turn northward and contact Donna. She adds a bunch of detail.

"Ok ladies, here's the scoop. Our target is on its way. Their new electronic security capabilities have somehow masked the boat itself from our view.   But their wake can still be picked up by SkyLock. Did they not think of that?   Of course we're assuming Skylock will detect the right wake on the basis that it will be the only wake not preceded by a boat outline. Very odd. See what I mean on the screen."

We watch a new satellite image invade the video screen. A number of boats are queued up waiting to pass through Dodd Narrows at both the NW and SE entrances. We zoom in on the northern approach, identifying five boats patiently waiting for their turn to proceed. Behind the fifth is indeed a very weak extra wake but no boat visible. Not even a blurry patch or pixelation disturbance.   Nothing indicates any vessel present. Sure is weird. We wonder what a following boat would think, coming up on a wake but seeing nothing to cause it. Assume something underwater is causing the disturbance we guess. Maybe the guys on board the drug cruiser circle around to always be in the last spot.

Donna provides a voice-over. "So the wake clearly prevents the ship from hiding totally from us. These smugglers are not dumb. I can't believe they haven't realized this. What are we missing? There's got to be something more. While our guys here think on it, your mission is to apprehend the boat as soon as it enters U.S. waters, same as always. I just know this baby is going to lead us a merry dance however. Keep in touch ladies, and good luck."

The *Sea-Thong* travels slowly southeast, running between Valdes and Reid Islands, then along Trincomali Channel. She slows at the southern tip of Galiano Island as a large B.C. ferry cuts across her path heading into Active Pass. Active Pass is an S shaped natural passageway about 3.5 miles long, bordered by Galiano and Mayne islands, connecting the protected inter-island

waters with the open Strait of Georgia. At its narrowest, the Pass is 2000 ft wide. Often the B.C. ferries running in opposite directions between Tsawwassen and Swartz Bay pass cautiously in the passage providing passengers a thrill given the proximity the respective captains manage.

Sea-Thong surprises us by following the B.C. ferry into the Pass, making us wonder if she's headed for Blaine, or Lummi Island in the U.S. It's Anna with her brilliant mind who deduces what's going on.

"These guys are smarter than we think," she announces. "Look, the B.C. ferry from Tsawwassen is coming into the Pass from the other direction at the same time. I bet *Sea-Thong* is going to pick one of the two ferries to follow. She'll tag along behind one of them, close enough that her wake will be swallowed up by that of the ferry whose coat-tails she hides behind."

Priscilla chimes in, a hint of urgency in her voice. "You got it girl. Amazing. Good thinking. We'd have to choose one of the ferries to shadow. What if we choose the wrong one? Kath, I think you need to contact Donna urgently and see if there's another team available to back us up. Damn these guys. They're good."

I tap my throat nodule. Donna answers immediately. I fill her in on what we're observing and Anna's thoughts. Anna yells loud enough for Donna to hear. "She's gone. The ferries have just passed and she's behind one of them. But which?" I pick up the thread. "Donna, can the

Point Roberts team get out there and watch for the smugglers boat to break away from the Tsawwassen ferry's course?"

Her answer is not encouraging. "Unfortunately that team is engaged in an exercise with the Canadian Mounties on Bowen Island. They'd never get back in time to do what you suggest. No I'll alert our folks in Blaine, Bellingham, and Lummi to get out in zodiacs and watch the waters. It's all I can do. You concentrate on watching for a breakaway wake behind the ferry headed to Swartz Bay. I suspect these folks must have more ideas up their sleeves. Far cleverer than any previous groups we've encountered. Out."

Right, easier said than done. The last spotty remnants of cloud-deflected sunlight have now sunk below the craggy outlines of the islands. A heavy cloud cover has arrived, taking the light almost totally away. Seeing any wake is becoming more difficult by the minute, although the interior lights behind the B.C. ferry windows shine through the haze. We maneuver 200 yards off the ship's port stern wondering if the smugglers are laughing at us from a position close-by in the ferry wake or alternatively laughing at us well north as they sail unescorted in the opposite direction.

Are we 'so near' or yet 'so far'?

Chapter 8. Tactics

It's time for Anna to come up with more brilliant predictions. If the smugglers are behind the southbound ferry it's clear they cannot follow her into Swartz Bay. The ferry dock there is not like Friday Harbor on San Juan Island where the dock is right beside a cove where the smugglers could hide. Anna checks the charts. We have our navigation lights on, but I tell Priscilla to turn them off so we are almost as invisible to the smugglers as they are to us, if indeed they are going our way.

Anna suggests they'll break away from the ferry wake as late as possible. Which means they'll probably head for an anchorage spot in a cove on one of the five islands to the east and south of Swartz Bay. As the ferry slows down for docking it will churn the waters behind its stern heavily, courtesy of the reversing props. That will be the best time for the smugglers to slip away. Especially if they do it very slowly. Phosphorescence from the ferry's reverse thrusts will make it difficult to see any ripples from a very light wake, especially given the poor light.

Priscilla challenges Anna. "Why do you think they'll stop for the night? Wouldn't it be smarter to keep going and slowly cross Haro Strait to some hiding place in the U.S. while they've got us all bamboozled? For all we know they're heading that way right this minute, while we sit here pontificating."

Anna replies matter-of-factly. "Good point Priscilla. Makes lots of sense. Save for one thing. Despite the pink clouds we saw late this afternoon, there's a massive storm brewing over the San Juan Islands. The Washington State ferries have ceased running already, the airports at Roche and Orcas are closed, and marinas throughout the area are busy ensuring all boats are made more secure at their docks, and shop owners are boarding up. Waves in Haro Strait are forecast at six feet, and our smuggler boys would be running smack against the direction they need to travel."

I add my two cents. "I guess we'll be somewhat protected if we stay in Swartz Bay while Coal and Goudge Islands to our east take the brunt of the onslaught."

Anna responds. "Yes, but I have a plan. Maybe we can chat over a light supper. I'm still hungry, even though that dinner at Sidney was superb."

We call and tell Donna where things are at. We dock in Swartz Bay, don't even try to find our target boat. Then share our frustrations over a bite at the port's cafeteria. Priscilla and I are anxious to hear Anna's plan.

"First," she says. "I think our target came this way, not towards the northern coastline. Way too open, less places to hide there. Was a cool move to choose the ferries crossing and making us uncertain. I'll give them credit for tying up our resources, but nothing more. These guys who've been hiding in front of us have also heard the weather forecast. If I were managing their precious cargo I would want a very protected cove to spend the night, which eliminates all those on the east side of the nearby islands.

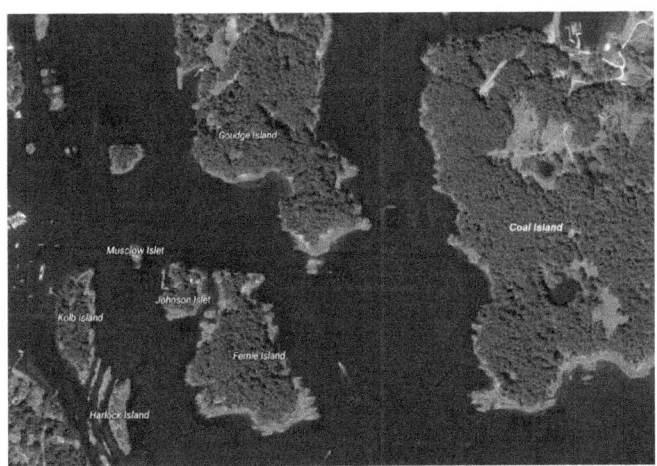

"Coal Island will undoubtedly take the brunt of the storm in this area. I think some of its northeast and southeast shorelines will take a severe beating. On the other hand Coal Island will help by smoothing down the waves for the other islands between it and the coast here. We'll mainly feel the wind rather than water turbulence.

"There's a large cove at the south end of Goudge Island where they could anchor, although I would choose a much smaller cove with less chance of wind swirls, maybe along Fernie Island's western shoreline. There are spots at the north end opposite Johnson Inlet and further south as well. Pretty good protection although I'd still have someone on watch all night to check the anchor didn't drag."

Sounds very reasonable to me, yet not enough. I let my frustration vent. "Still doesn't help us find the creeps does it if they've got their electronic shield up?" We've relied so heavily on overhead drone eyes in all our previous busts that it's bugging me that we're thwarted this time.

Maybe I'm getting tired of the chase and the job, because I feel totally helpless. Not a good sign. I rest my chin in my hands, annoyed at my feelings and my incompetence. Priscilla senses my state of mind, and punches me playfully on my left arm. "Come on boss, we can still follow their wake in the morning. Don't get down."

Anna speaks up. "Maybe, maybe not. If they suspect we're on to them, and even if not, I think they'll be very cautious. Because of the very point you make. They know their wake will show."

"So what will they do?" I ask Anna.

"If I were piloting their boat, here's what I would do. Use the same ruse again. The storm that's about to be upon us will be violent but short. By morning, the wind will have dropped off markedly, although it will still be blowing, and raining at the same time. The seas in Haro Strait will be down to 2 feet. They could move south at very slow speed from whatever cove they are in overnight and stop at Sidney Spit. With the wind still fierce it would be hard to pick up their wake going there."

Priscilla is confused. "Why head for Sidney rather than get out of Canadian waters?"

I finally catch up with Anna's mental prowess. "Same ruse! I get it. Follow in the wake of the Sidney to Anacortes ferry that leaves around noon, and once in U.S. waters slip away in one of the narrow passages it passes through. Shit, Anna, I hope you never join the other side. Smart thinking."

Priscilla leans back, points to shore where the Madrona trees are already bending before the wind. "Shit is right. How the 'F' do we catch these creeps?"

Anna smiles. "How do you feel about taking a swim later tonight Kath?"

My eyes open wide. What the heck is she talking about? "Huh?" is all I can manage in response. Priscilla raises her eyebrows and we both look at Anna for clarification.

"I've been thinking about this new electronic fence they've managed to arrange. I can't imagine it extends underwater. So what if we did a little night prowling in appropriate coves using those power scooters we have in the inside locker? We swim underwater using the new infrared flashlights, whose beams can't be seen from above, and whenever we come across a power boat keel we pop up to see if there's an associated superstructure visible. If not, we've identified our Azimut."

"Brilliant!" I exclaim. Priscilla's head is nodding up and down in amazement. She yabbers excitedly. "And there's a new device I just heard about that will help us enormously. Listen to this. It's a fancy type of underwater location transmitter. Obviously not like a GPS transponder. Rather, it's a palm-sized device that sends out coded alert sounds which can be picked up by a special underwater receiver. It's a small-scale version of what the navy submarine boys use to track debris from broken-up ships, like containers for example. The devices they use are huge and much more sophisticated but the ones I read about will work fine for our purposes.

"Once you find the Azimut you simply attach the device below the transom and above the rudder. It's battery powered, undetectable by ordinary electronic sensors, and sends out a signal for about 50 hours. Battery technology has advanced remarkably in the last fifteen years. We'd have only gotten 5 hours way back. Fifty hours should give us plenty of time for tracking, and hopefully apprehending."

Anna leans forward. "Are there any of these devices on board? I don't recollect seeing any."

"Unfortunately not," Priscilla answers. "But let me send off a drone to HQ and get a couple. If that wind across the Strait is not too strong yet it should be back in 45 minutes or so."

She texts Donna with her request, then adjusts the settings for one of the four prowlers in the hangars on the front deck. With a solid whoosh it heads into the night skies. Usually just used for photographic reconnaissance, the drones also come in handy for tasks just like this.

For long distance deliveries we use Umbridge Services group. They have high-level security clearance. It's fascinating to see one of their big machines hover 100 feet above us then dispatch a smaller drone to our deck with whatever parcel is destined for us.

From being a bit down not that long ago, I'm now up and energized. We sit down together and map out the coves we think are the most likely hiding spots the smugglers might select. When done I fetch our wetsuits and the underwater scooters, check over the newly arrived Underwater Pulse Units (UPUs) and submerge the associated receiver on its long pole at the starboard stern.

Each of us is good at many pursuits. I have the edge in swimming and diving, followed closely by Anna. Hence our election for what could be a long, cold exercise. And for all we know, a potentially fruitless one.

We've made a lot of assumptions. That the smuggler's boat is in the vicinity, that it will indeed hole-up for the night to avoid the storm, and that there is nothing making the underwater hull undiscoverable. We've made mistakes before, but part of our attitude is to try all we can, until there are no options left. Only then would we call for reinforcements.

I wonder if we'll find anything useful tonight.

Chapter 9. On target

The water is cold. Damned cold. Priscilla has taken us within
100 yards of our first destination cove. Before we rolled off
the rubber skirt we identified anchor lights on four boats.
Three of them are also showing interior cabin lights. Anna
and I split at the cove entrance. I head off on a clockwise
rotation, Anna heads anticlockwise. We duck dive and swim
underwater, the scooters giving us about 3 knots of speed.
Our watches are synchronized to help us pop up and check
for each other at ten minute intervals.

That's the hard part, finding each other in the dark. Our
adaptive masks with their night vision viewing capabilities
work well if pointed in the right direction. And even though
we both felt good about our orientation when sitting on the
boat fender, the world looks quite different at sea-level. We
meet up for the third time at the thirty minute point, our
mission unsuccessful. I activate the laser signal which allows
Priscilla to home in on us, arriving in two minutes flat.

We climb aboard, tell our sad tale, and check our tanks' air
supplies as Priscilla heads for target cove #2. There are many
more boats in this cove as it is much wider than the first
cove. It looks like several boats have stern-tied to shore as
deck lights reflect off nylon lines stretching between boat
and the tree-line. There seem to be two significant gaps
between groups of boats, so we agree to explore those first,
then move to the boats lit up that are anchored much closer
to each other. Anna's hopeful that one of the gaps may hold
our target in hiding, but I think we're more likely to find it in
some cove more protected.

Despite our best efforts we end up drawing another blank,
and are starting to feel a little tired from our exertions. We

steel ourselves to try one more time, although there are two coves still to search. Priscilla, with her excellent vision, unerringly takes us to the next cove. There's a reflection off strips of metal junk on an old unused pier to one side of the cove. Makes me wonder if quartz was mined there in ancient days or a long gone small resort once existed there. The cove is tiny enough that just one of us could make the search alone, but for safety we decide to both go. This time we swim together.

Starting near the pier we circle anticlockwise about four feet below the surface. We haven't gone twenty feet when Anna grabs my arm and pushes me away as she encounters a huge rock almost directly in front of her. It's as big as a hut, emerging silently from the sea-floor 10 feet below us. Scary. We motor on, a bit more cautiously. Maybe the place is strewn with large rocks which is why no one has anchored here. We've gone three quarters of the way around when Anna stops, and holds me back. We're swimming beside one another and she's closest to land. She turns to her right and glides slowly towards an indistinct dark shape. This is no rock rising from below but a man-made shape drooping from above.

No question about it, it's the sleek hull on a large boat. We can see the massive 30" props up close. Has to be our target, anchored in a very risky place. Had they scoped this out beforehand I wonder? I cautiously poke my head above water.

It's as if I've gone blind. There is nothing to see. Nada, rien, zilch. How can they do that? To test my senses I go underwater again and swim to the stern. Careful not to make any noise I run my hand up the transom. My hand keeps touching smooth fiberglass above the water surface proving the boat is indeed floating there. Amazing! It suddenly registers that I may be putting us at risk. What if there's an alarm system associated with the screening? I hastily pull my hand back under water. Anna looks at me quizzically. I signal everything is OK.

She retrieves the two UPUs from her pants leg pocket, and attaches them to either side of the prop shafts housings. Nice to see an old-fashioned prop arrangement still being used instead of the more modern IPS prop units. I chastise myself for thinking anything positive about a smuggler boat, and turn away, the two of us making for open water where we stop and high-five, then continue on our way.

Priscilla is thrilled with our news and I can't help reiterating my thanks to Anna for her brilliant strategic thinking. Lots of her assumptions have just been validated. Maybe this gal should join the research sleuths who are the intelligentsia of our security forces. I have the feeling though that she likes this operational work. At least for now.

It's time for us to hunker down back in Swartz Bay for the night, but first Anna and I need to warm up. Hot showers are in demand. In light of her incredible deductions I let Anna go first while I shiver away wrapped in a couple of towels. After a couple of minutes she yells, "Kath, can you please pass me my hairbrush? It's on the bed in my cabin. I forgot it damn it."

No problem. I'm sure her hair is tangled like mine from our tight wet suit caps. I find the brush easily enough and open the bathroom door. Steam pours out of the enclosure. Anna is pressed up against the acrylic shower door, her arm stretched over the top waiting for the brush.

I'm already feeling good from the euphoria associated with our cove find. Seeing Anna's gorgeous body creates an extra thrill that runs up and down my frame. She makes a gentle pass with the brush through her fiery red ringlets. I watch her perfectly mounded breasts rise and fall, and focus on her snatch rubbing up and down against the door. I guess I had expected to see pubes in red, but she presents her vulva unadorned. I lift my eyes but she hasn't missed anything.

She smiles knowingly and mouths, "Keep watching." I do, appreciating some bewitching gyrations and exposures until I find myself grabbing my crotch. Oh my! Clit control definitely required. I reluctantly turn and leave.

Chapter 10. Anticipation

The wind howls, and the rain pours buckets on the cockpit roof and side windows. We rock rhythmically, even though we're tied very securely to the dock. Our rubber fenders screech as they rub against the pier, and the rope lines creak as they tighten and slacken with our every move. I've slept fitfully for three hours, but have decided the tossing and turning in the cramped quarters is sending me a message. I get up, use the head, then pull heavy winter pants and jacket over my pyjamas, and peek out the companionway door.

Given the way we are docked, the rain is sweeping from bow to stern, so I pop up and take a cockpit seat looking backwards at the deluge soaking everything in sight. Flags on the dockyard mast are tearing at the end, and trees are bent to the wind's shaping interests. I wonder how birds fare in this kind of gale. Must find protected places or they'd be blown away to a new location.

A new sound registers. I turn and find Priscilla coming through the hatchway. Moreover, she's holding two cups of coffee. Wisps of steam coil upwards, adding to the delight I anticipate. She too is in winter gear, but has smartly tied a scarf around her head as well. Why didn't I think of that? She hands over a cup, a smile on her lips. "This should help," she says as she sits close beside me, adding warmth. I thank her and hold the cup with both hands, heating them simultaneously.

I share some information. "I managed to get a lengthy report off to Donna, before I fell asleep. Knowing her, she's probably read it already. Such a night owl. I'm sure she'll be excited at our underwater findings."

The wind surges and a new thought hits me. "I wonder how the boats in Roche Harbor marina are surviving this mess. They have some huge vessels making their home there. Do you think the marina notifies owners ahead of time about pending storms like this?"

Priscilla responds knowingly. "Actually, I think the marina contacts the local boat services companies that take care of the boats for the remote owners. It's in the marina's interest to make sure everything is lashed down tightly. Even so I bet there'll be minor damage. Some of those maintenance companies are not as professional and diligent as others. I know. Worked for one of them one summer. Fun job. I still remember one of the young chaps on the team. Philip was his name. We tested a couple of the king-sized beds in the VIP staterooms. He had more moves than someone on that old TV show – 'dancing with the stars'. Wonder what he's doing now."

Priscilla smiles as she continues. "I love making out with guys who treasure their bodies and who have a penchant for sharing two way. Harder to find these days. Have we emasculated them all Kath? Sometimes I wonder if our woman's world has moved the pendulum too far from a midpoint of balance."

I nod, but keep my thoughts to myself. Musing over my own flirtations years ago. Unique experiences tend to stay in my mind. A few more crowd in. Fun travel destinations and activities, first prom dress, arguments with my father, hurt at being dumped by a boyfriend, champion tennis trophy, a car crash that was my fault, loss of a girlfriend because of a huge lie I told, indistinct other memories.

I stop thinking, stand, and walk towards the stern but stay under cover. Deliberately turn my mind to the situation at hand. "Here's a thought for you Priscilla. Clearly Anna has identified the drug boys' strategy and mindset. I'm inclined to buy her notion that they'll use the Sidney to Anacortes ferry wake again tomorrow. Instead of trying to follow these guys using the UPUs in the morning, what if we get out of here and hide along the ferry route and wait for them to come by?"

"Makes sense Kath. Anna hasn't been wrong yet. Getting ahead of the smugglers means there's no chance they'll see us until it's too late. In fact maybe we should even hide by Roche so they won't spot us trailing them across Haro Strait. Once they're on the U.S. side of the border it's Game On! When they come in sight, we could run ahead of them so they think we're just out trolling, and as soon as they turn off the ferry route to deliver their goods we could close in. Where's Anna? We need to share this plan. It's solid."

I like the idea. I should, I created a large part of it. We both head back to bed but I set the alarm for a 4:30 am wake-up, hoping that the forecast is correct for continued rain but a major drop in wind gustiness.

I knock on Anna's door at 4:45 am and hear her stir in response. 15 minutes later over coffee and toast Priscilla and I detail our new idea. She's all for it. Asks if we've gotten the weather forecast. We have. The wind has already dropped, although not as much as expected, and it is still raining. It will be a rough ride across the Strait with 3 ft seas, the waves running against us. Anna thinks of one more check. Is the ferry from Anacortes to Sidney still planning to run? It's the return trip we're concerned about, but if the ferry doesn't make the outbound run, both we and the drug peddlers will need an alternate plan.

All the ferry officials must still be asleep in Anacortes as no one answers my call. So we contact our local Homeland team there. A bright voice assures us that the tail end of the storm is just passing through their town and the talker sees no reason for any of the ferry schedules to be inoperative. Very reassuring.

Priscilla volunteers to go outside and get wet releasing the lines holding us tight against the dock. It takes longer than usual as we had used extra lines, and doubly reinforced them around the dock cleats. The outboards spring to life with a vibrant snarl, probably waking neighbors. At Priscilla's thumbs-up sign I use the bow thruster to ease us off the windy pier. The boat fights the wind for an instant, so I reverse the port prop and the added torque moves us clear.

We maneuver south at 5 knots. It feels like we are crawling. But we get a boost when we pass the cove where our target boat is hiding and we pick up the twin signals from the UPUs. At least the smugglers haven't left their spot yet. Encouraging.

Beyond the protection of Coal Island the wind hits us with renewed force. We get blown sideways, so I have no choice but to increase speed and turn easterly directly into the path of the storm. Even in the ultra poor light we can see whitecaps stretching before us. I turn to the girls. "Sure you want to do this? We are going to get bounced around like flotsam, and well and truly washed if we proceed."

"Let's do it," Anna yells. "Go for it," Priscilla adds. I turn on the two high-powered searchlights on our arch, focus one 75 yards out, the other just 20 yards in front, give their controls to Anna.

I ask Priscilla to focus on the close-in light, and to give warning of anything in our path. In this part of the world, forestry and logging are still highly remunerative occupations. Second growth forests are felled, and the logs floated south in huge raft arrangements to various saw mills. It's not unusual for logs to break free from the log-jams, and floating logs are a sailor's nightmare. Especially in rapids where they can act like spears thrown upwards by swirling currents and drive holes in the hulls of even decent-sized boats. Putting rapids aside, just hitting a free-floating log can be dangerous. If it is partially submerged and damages a prop, one of the more common collisions, a journey can become a disaster very quickly.

Especially after a violent storm, like the one whose tail-end we are still experiencing, there's bound to be plenty of logs tossed loose. I don't want to hit one. Haro Strait is ten miles wide where we are attempting to cross in darkness. We plough into the melee at 12 knots, breaking through white caps, water washing over the bow almost constantly. The rain beats upon the windshield and the wipers have little effect. We strain to see but keep our eyes glued on the waves coming at us. At some point we actually cross the border, that invisible line in the water which, in our view, attracts far too many people with ill-founded intentions.

We've each found an appropriate bracing position that helps us manage the continuous up and down motion. A large freighter looms out of the darkness. If we'd been watching the radar we would have seen it earlier but all eyes are in survival mode checking what's immediately ahead in the field of vision defined by the big spotlights. The cargo vessel has all its lights on. Not just its navigation beacons but also the huge floodlights on vertical poles between the hatches that help loading and unloading at night. It crosses our path maybe 200 yards ahead, like a ghost in a fantasy scene. It scares me that we weren't sufficiently alert to be watching the radar as well as our path forward. And why didn't they issue a warning? I take it upon myself to be more diligent.

There's no conversation. We're all tense, managing progress on a minute by minute basis. We have faith in the boat – she probably handles the elements better than we do. Three quarters of the way across we see a faint patch of grey in the sky. A small gap between heavy, low overcast clouds. It disappears as quickly as it catches our attention, but it's a positive sign. First sense of the light of daybreak in our 55 minutes of travel. Even though blackness returns, we're encouraged. We plough on.

The chartplotter finally chimes when we're 100 yards north of Battleship Island. Time to turn southeast and head carefully into the marina at Roche Harbor. I let out a thankful sigh, and the girls grin. They feel the relief too.

Docking is a challenging task with the wind wanting to place us in a berth contrary to where we want to tie up. But we prevail. A quick call to HQ finds the office open, so we don wet weather gear and hasten along the narrow dock walkways, hanging on to one another to counter the wind. Donna turns up 30 minutes after we arrive and we share our stories and latest ideas with her. She's supportive, although raises the notion that the *Sea-Thong* may try to cross Haro Strait early, just like we did. It would be hard to pick up her wake given the turbulent waters.

Her argument has some value, so we reluctantly pack up, put our foul weather gear back on and trudge back to our boat. In case Donna is right there's no value in staying in the marina. Instead, we make a quick run to Neil Bay, just north of Roche's main harbor, and close to the Anacortes/Sidney ferry route. Only problem is that the bay opens to the east so at anchor there we would be facing into the wind, rocking badly, and not looking westward to watch the ferry coming back across the strait. There is no bay facing westward in the vicinity, so we have no good choice.

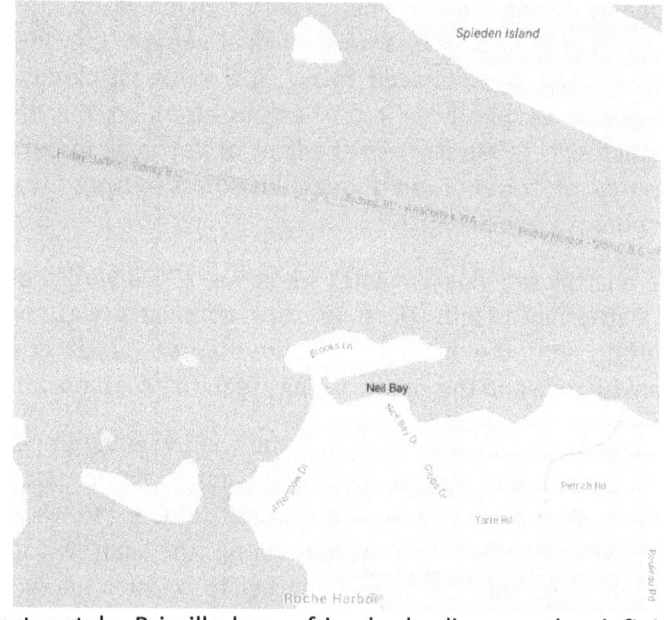

Fortunately, Priscilla has a friend who lives on the defining peninsula with a private dock reaching out into the north side of the bay. Priscilla calls, and finds the woman's husband has taken their powerboat down to Seattle for repairs, so she is happy to allow us to tie up instead of anchoring. Very helpful, although we still won't have a direct line of sight to the west.

Our ears are on, as we say, but we detect no UPU signal in the following three hours.

Around 10:45 am the Anacortes to Sidney ferry steams past going west, black smoke billowing from her funnel and racing ahead of her. It looks strange. The rain is now down to a drizzle so we can see fairly easily. If the ferry runs on time coming back, allowing for heavy seas, she should be in our vicinity just before 1 pm. We decide we'll pull out into the Speiden Channel around 12:45 pm so that we'll be visible to both the ferry and *Sea-Thong* hopefully trailing behind her.

Our excitement bubbles over in nervous chatter as we wait. We're in our home waters, the storm is easing, and so far, everything has worked fine. We're ready to nab these turkeys. Come on *Sea-Thong*!

Chapter 11.   Closing in

The ferry is late. No real surprise, she's ploughing through waves fueled by a stiff breeze. Gradually her frame becomes larger, but she's still a mile away. We each have on headphones, waiting not so patiently to detect the first beeps from the underwater transmitters on our target boat. The wind swirls around our windows adding noise we don't need. Where are they? Come on guys, show up!

Anna picks up a faint sound, cocks her head and furrows her brows. She raises her hand to signal she needs full quiet from us. The woman has hearing as sensitive as a bat's. I trust it implicitly. I watch her face closely. Ten seconds drift by. I hold my breath.

She smiles and raises her thumb in jubilation. "Got 'em," she mouths. We swap high fives. Priscilla starts nodding her head. She's hearing them now too. I take off my headphones. We'll let Anna keep track of the smugglers.

They're in U.S. waters now so we have every right to intercept them. Except for the problem that we can't see them. Nor their wake. Patience, patience, patience needed. At some point they'll turn off course and we'll follow them. We've talked about how to proceed at that point, but our action may depend on the location they select. We'll see.

My supposition is that they will go all the way to Anacortes. It's a good-sized town and has access to mainland road and rail transportation.   Anna thinks differently. She argues that the smugglers would have to ease out from behind the ferry before it makes its final southward turn towards the Anacortes docks, and then head for a cove or Skyline Marina. Plenty of distance to have their wake seen.

She thinks Orcas Island is a better bet. The ferry has to pass through narrow passages as it heads eastward, and the island offers three good harbors with small coves where it could anchor. Goods could be transferred to a truck which would take one of the smaller inter-island ferries to the mainland.

I'm beginning to think Anna must have some extra experience about the subtle options of navigating through the islands. She's got insight I don't have. She offers a new thought.

"We know they're coming. There's no way they'll risk stopping around this area where we are since it's a major base for U.S. Customs, so they have to go further along the ferry route. Why don't we leave now, way ahead of them. They won't see us, so we avoid giving them any hint that we might know what they are doing."

Priscilla asks, "OK, makes sense, but where will we hide along the way?"

"The ferry will pass slowly through Wasp Passage, which is only 1000 feet wide at its narrowest. Plenty of depth though – 90 feet. I think we should sit just off the northeastern shore of McConnell Island, where we'll be able to see the ferry coming southeast from Speiden and also watch it in the passage."

I'm concerned. "There are dangerous reefs among those small Wasp Islands Anna. Is there somewhere else we could sit and wait?"

"Not that would give us as the same double outlook, Kath. Our charts are up to date. We should be fine."

"Well, if you say so. I just know that Vessel Assist pulled two boats off Yellow Island rocks this summer."

"We'll be well away from Yellow Island Kath, believe me."

"OK, let's get going then before it's too late."

Fifteen minutes later we're in our new location. We're all frustrated at the lack of action. We've been trailing these guys for what seems days, being incredibly patient, adjusting our strategy as we go, bearing up through challenging conditions, and acting blind most of the time. It's time for our meager efforts to pay off. Priscilla has offered a number of action-related thoughts but comes up with another that I think may be worth pursuing.

"If we really think they might be pulling in to Orcas Island somewhere, can we get SkyLock to look for any unusual truck activity. For example, a U-Haul rental sitting on a dead-end road near a cove or a boat ramp. May mean nothing. May give us a clue."

I pass this request on to Donna, who says she'll get in touch with SkyLock authorities.

Twenty minutes later the ferry comes into view and we pick up the UPU alerts again. Good, our target hasn't deserted us along the way. We all tense up, our senses maximized for eliciting information that might lead to action. We watch as the ferry starts its turn to the left to enter Wasp Passage. I realize I've crossed my fingers in anticipation, and release them. The ferry disappears behind Crane Island, but we still hear the UPU alerts coming through our speakers steadily. They fade as the smugglers dip behind Crane as well.

We move slowly off our mark heading for the top of Crane Island, intending to pass south through Pole Pass and pick up the trail again.

Out of the blue Anna yells urgently, "Kath, hold it." I throttle back quickly and turn towards her. She motions dead ahead, then points to her headset. "They're here, they've left the ferry and have come north through Pole Pass. They must be heading for Deer Harbor. Look, you can see their wake."

"At last. We've finally got the bastards!" I shout.

Chapter 12. Encounter

"But they can't avoid seeing us now, we're in plain sight, there's no more than 500 yards between us," Priscilla exclaims. "What the shit do we do?"

"Keep calm," I respond. "They think they are still unseen, and if we stay still they may conclude it's just coincidence that we're here. I can well imagine them thinking that no-one could have guessed in advance what route they'd take. But, so saying, I have an idea which will probably change all that."

"What?" Priscilla asks.

"Let's launch one of the drones, and see if it can cut through their electronic defensive shield, forcing a breakdown. The question is whether the smugglers will hear the drone or see it. If they do they'll know we are on to them. Does one of the drones have a metal proximity sensor on board that can govern tracking?"

Anna jumps in. "Drone #4 has the latest stealth technology incorporated. Nearly silent, different infrastructure profile. I can have it on its way in 15 seconds and adjust its course as soon as its aloft. Is it a go?"

"Yes, do it." I don't hesitate, although I wonder what the smugglers will do if my idea works.

We wait in baited silence. Then I realize we haven't yet let headquarters know. I sit on the back settee and have a quick conversation with Donna. I tell her to get land forces moving from our East Sound office to the shoreline by Deer Harbor Rd. Trouble is, that's a two-man office. She promises to use a helicopter out of Anacortes to bring reinforcements.

The stealth drone has built-in intelligence. It's sending back GPS signals that indicate it's 20 feet above the water and flying in elongated ovals, clearly aligning with the smugglers' boat path as it moves northward. While the satellites can't capture images through the electronic shielding, the drone must be responding to the metal railings and other metal devices on the boat, as hoped. I love technology when it works. We should have tried this option earlier.

"OK Anna, bring it down to flybridge level, but let's be prepared. If this works, the crooks will know we're on to them immediately. And someone on the fly bridge may be fast enough to shoot the machine down."

Priscilla engages the system for the machine gun mounted on the bow pulpit, and places laser driven rifles beside each of us. I reach down to pick mine up.

There's a metallic ping on the deck near the bow and a bullet ricochets into the port windshield, shattering it into tiny fragments. Clearly our drone has been discovered. And consequently we have just become a major threat. But has the drone done what I wanted? Is their boat now visible? I can't tell because Priscilla pulls me down under cover just as two more shots ping, one

catching the horn device above the starboard window and making it dangle in front of us.

Too darned close! I contact Donna and tell her our location and that we're under attack. I grab the remote dashboard control unit, advance the throttles to maximum and head northeast on an intercept path. More shots hit us, spraying wildly. In 12 seconds we cut the distance between us and the smugglers in half. Priscilla fires the bow gun using her handheld control, and GPS coordinates from the drone, aiming 10 feet below the drone's latest vertical position. It's a blind shot. We don't know if it works. Our boat reverberates with the intense sounds of the gun and the outboards.

Gingerly, I poke my head above the console. To my delight, the whole smuggler ship is visible. As much as it holds the bad guys, it is indeed a pretty craft. Very sleek. It's like a ghost coming out of hiding.

"We can see them," I yell. "Great job Anna. Good shooting Priscilla, there are small holes all along the port hull. Give 'em another burst!"

Two men are on the back deck, aiming rifles at us, the motion of their boat contributing to the inaccuracy of their shots. Another is watching us, empty-handed, from the flybridge. And we can see one more inside piloting the boat. Four total that we know about. More hidden below? Possibly, we can't be sure. Those we can see duck as the machine gun opens up again. More holes appear along their hull.

This is war! We're drawing closer second by second. At 100 yards out I use the hailer, ordering them to stop, and put down their weapons. To no avail. They swerve through a starboard 45 degree angle towards shore, aiming for a private jetty. I slow down and turn the same amount to port so we are running parallel 75 yards away.

"Rifles," I command. "Priscilla, the driver; Anna, the chap upstairs. I'll take the back deck." Priscilla sights her laser guide spot and fires first, an instant kill. The driver slumps sideways and the boat slams into the dock. Bits of wood fly through the air. Tormented wrenching sounds assault our ears. The boat's bow rises four feet, exposing the keel, pauses, then slides back into the water. The engines keep running, making the props churn the water to foam. One of the men at the back end is thrown over the transom, in danger of being cut to pieces by the props. The other slips and his rifle jerks out of his arms. My laser sight lights up his left arm, but my bullet misses as the boat rolls slightly towards shore on its long axis. I have no real target. The chap upstairs falls out of his chair, panics, and starts to climb down the stairs to the deck. Anna's shot is true. I watch the green laser circle on his vest turn to crimson. He loosens his hold on the railing and plummets to the deck. The engines finally stall and shut down. Smoke rises around the back deck.

We coast up to the multi million dollar mess, standing ten yards off. The chap thrown in the water is thrashing his way to shore, lucky to be alive. We let him go, anticipating our ground unit will arrive soon and catch him.

That's our first mistake. The second is ignoring the second chap on the back deck. The third mistake is the worst of all. Because suddenly our boat is raked with machine gun fire coming from three different spots. The shooters are on land, on both sides of a boat shed and behind a tree in the backyard of the house whose dock has just been ruined. Members of an unloading crew providing an unexpected reception, totally overlooked in all of our thinking.

We have no idea how many land-based smugglers exist, but that's too much firepower to fight by ourselves. We need help. I'm hoping our boat is still in working order, although I know one of the outboards is dead, as I see steam rising from it. Might have shielded the others due to the position we're holding. As I prepare to retreat by moving away fast, the chap on the Azimut's back deck we've forgotten about shoots. I hear the bullet's zing, and turn to see Anna clutching her throat, blood spilling through her fingers from what looks like a deep graze.

"Priscilla, help Anna," I yell, my attention focused on ensuring a fast getaway. Another shot whistles through the cabin's interior space before I finally haul ass out of there. I zig zag at speed trying to make us a difficult target. I head northwards along the shoreline and soon am out of the shooter's direct line of sight. I feel better.

Far too scary a situation. I quickly check on Anna, then call Donna. Tell her to hold the local team back, as they are heading for trouble.

We have one thing in our favor. The smugglers' boat is going nowhere. The urgency is to get troops to its location before the smugglers' unloading group can disperse and hide the drugs throughout the island, before moving them on at a later date.

Chapter 13. Massive haul

Anna will be fine Priscilla assures me. Antibiotic cream has been applied to the cleaned-up graze and one of the electronic medicated healing units placed over the wound. The first aid unit has been sending diagnostic information to the medical control center, and has already given her an injection to offset infection, help the wound heal, and calm her down. Had the bullet trajectory been a half inch to the right, she would be looking at more than a simple skin mark in the future. She's in a minimal state of shock, irritated and angry, but is coping well, her voice surprisingly unaffected. She asks, "What happened to the drone?" The drone's control unit has gone dark, so we presume the machine is underwater somewhere, it's mission fulfilled.

Priscilla and I inspect our boat looking for bullet holes and damaged components. The front deck is a disaster. The starboard hull has many holes, all well above the water line thank heavens. The arch has a series of dents, the base of one of the antennas is split in two, the antenna stretching backwards. A starboard window in the cockpit is blown to smithereens and one of the stateroom windows downstairs is cracked. The starboard-most outboard will never run again. I crawl into the space below the floorboards holding a high intensity flashlight. I see only one hole in the hull and then a clear water line that is leaking slowly. A small casualty I can temporarily fix with a repair sleeve and strong duct tape. I'm pleased to note nothing else seems

 problematic, although I know the marine mechanics will do a much better job of checking when we finally return to Roche. I'm surprised we got off so lightly. The boys at the house with machine guns must have been amateurs, generally firing too high, or outside our frame.

Our quick survey completed I transfer audio to our main screen so we can all listen in to the activity going on. Two helicopters have been launched from Anacortes. Their downward pointing cameras show them crossing Blakely Island. Each machine is carrying twelve combat soldiers. Apparently the transports are planning to land on Deer Harbor Rd., since it will take too long to get permission to use a nearby farmer's field. They'll be no more than 300 yards from where the smugglers are holed up. We're happy to be away from what can only become a nasty shootout.

The olive colored machines land and the marines run towards the house where the drug kings are. We hear gun fire and a few voice commands, but the views from the soldiers' helmet cameras are not passed on to us. In ten minutes all the noise ceases. It's obviously over. The local security force commander provides a terse summary. "Four men on the boat, two dead, thank you ladies. Six ground personnel, one dead, two seriously wounded about to be medivac'd, three surrendered. One seems to be the leader, but that's not clear at this moment. Treatment at prison HQ will soon produce the information we need. Another chopper is on the way so we can transport all the bad boy personnel off the island

Four of my men will remain, guarding the house and the boat, and securing the drugs. Local police will keep spectators away from the area. Looks like an incredible haul – several hundred million dollars' worth by our initial estimates. Thank you all for an excellent operation and result. Update in 30 minutes. Out."

Sort of disappointing in a way that we girls aren't there at the end to see it all wrapped up. We're all curious to learn more, so I retrace our path a little ways offshore back to the house, where we anchor 50 yards out. I call Donna and ask her to patch me through to the leading soldier onsite.

He quickly joins the call. "Lieutenant Carmichael here. How can I help you ma'am?" He walks out the back door and takes a few steps along a pathway towards the damaged dock and waves at us.

I ask, "We'd like to see things up close Lieutenant if possible. It's been a tough exercise for us."

"No problem ma'am. Come on by. Just stay clear of the dock. We're not sure how safe it and the damaged boat are."

Anna elbows me hard in the ribs, a pair of binoculars dangling from her other hand. "Did you see that hulk?" she exclaims. "Man oh man. If we're headed that way I'm taking my StatVibe. Did you see that mound in his khakis?"

I shake my head. One minute the gal is entertaining me from her shower, the next minute she's eyeing some guy's hidden attributes. Guess we know her tastes. Bi, like Priscilla. Lingering questions now answered. Anna heads to the downstairs cabin and returns with a black cloth pouch.

The StatVibe is a sex-toy. Pretty ingenious I must admit. It euphemistically provides the latest in 'male physique intelligence,' 'guaranteed to simulate what a full readiness position might offer, in high def video.' Anna is already strapping the gadget to her wrist. It has the form of an old fashioned watch. The skin-colored hold-clips have some sort of flexible biometric magnets that conform to anyone's wrist almost instantly. On the inside of the device there is a flat video screen possibly 1.5" by 1", and a single push button at one end. It can clearly be used very discreetly.

Priscilla is watching as Anna straps it on. I can tell she is dying to see it in action. She's been incredibly vocal about men's 'appointments', as she calls them, ever since I've known her, more than three years now. "It's not length," she'd say. "We only have a max 5 inches available. It's girth that matters gals. How filled we can be. You don't want something that doesn't touch the sides." Anna hints that her new toy will yield accurate measurements and projections of male genitals as long as the target is within 5 feet. The manufacturers promise longer focal lengths, knowing the current version is

somewhat limited in its usefulness. She asks for our help in managing a close up shot of Carmichael's offerings.

We tie the zodiac up to a sloping rock wall and scramble to the top. The back yard has a small grove of fruit trees whose limbs and trunks have been torn asunder. The boat shed has collapsed in one corner, and the lawn is churned up from bullets and heavy boots. One large fir tree is pockmarked with bullet holes. There's blood on the door frame of the house, and empty shell casings all over the place. A small invasion has clearly taken place.

We see two men carefully unloading the Azimut as Carmichael comes forward to greet us. He has a commanding presence. Must be 6ft 4in, with massive chest and forearms, craggy face, thin dark hair, thick legs joined bulkily. He offers his congratulations, the tail end of his speech drowned out as the extra helicopter swoops by. He looks up and Anna gets her shot.

I'd love to see the dashboard on the smugglers' boat and see how their controls are set up, even play with them. Anna and Priscilla are more interested to see what type of vermin we tracked. They are led to the captives' holding room. A downcast motley lot don't even lift their heads at the new visitors. Priscilla asks in Spanish "Who shot down our drone?" She gets a blank stare in return, and mutters under her breath, "You bunch of fucking murderers. Glad we got you. Enjoy our underground pigsties." Anna grabs her arm and pulls her away, a tad worried that Priscilla's anger might overflow.

We hang around until the soldiers in the latest helicopter turn up. They are all business, dismissing our presence with harsh glances signaling us to get out of their way. Which we do. As we head back across the lawn to our zodiac Donna calls. We're ordered to take our boat back to Anacortes, rather than Roche, for repairs, and to stay there until notified about our next assignment. We're scheduled to debrief at the office the next morning and are told that nearby hotel reservations have been made in our names.

Back on board our trusty vessel, Anna insists we follow her into the downstairs cabin to view the StatVibe capture out of the sunlight. The resolution on Anna's wrist image is remarkable. Carmichael's crown jewels are silhouetted in stark black and white. Perhaps a little larger than most men's of his age, but nothing like some late teenagers' offerings we'd all seen. "Pretty standard," I suggested.

"Maybe, let's see," Anna responds. "It'll take a few seconds to bring up the 'aroused' projection images and measurements when I hit the switch. Don't be impatient."

I don't know how many millions of data points IBM must have analyzed in order to provide some small porn-data company the appropriate information for their algorithms, but the resultant image of a phallus at 7.0" length and 5.75" inches girth is definitely titillating. Hot stuff. Both measurements are deemed to be within the 95th percentile of comparative data. I believe it.

The image shuts down as Anna twists her wrist, and we stare at each other marveling at the advanced technology we've just seen in action. Not just technology. More honestly, technology plus anatomy. Anna is reflective. "Hmmm, I wonder if he might be free for drinks tonight. I'll call Donna and see if she has a contact number. Might have to leave you two to fend for yourselves I'm afraid."

We head for Anacortes, short one engine. On the way, we clean up shards of glass on the furniture and floor of the cockpit, poke out the broken windows, and tie in place odd hanging bits and pieces. Our baby is a mess. We wonder whether she'll she ever feel the same.

As we walk into the big meeting room at HQ there are loud cheers and shouts of 'Well done', 'Super heroes', 'Massive haul', 'Congratulations', 'Great catch', and more. I blush a little, for we all feel we were just doing our job. Probably undervaluing what we accomplished however. The drug haul is the largest in history and a truly super prize. The captured boat becomes U.S. property now, a grand addition to our fleet. While the boat itself has high value, the electronic systems in place on it are even more rewarding. This boat carries state-of-the art anti-detection systems more advanced than our current systems. I imagine the security geeks can hardly contain their enthusiasm to check her over. Happy to have arranged delivery men!

Amazing what we three gals can do!

www.ingramcontent.com/pod-product-compliance
Lightning Source LLC
Chambersburg PA
CBHW072358030726
47505CB00014B/1884